RS Ø3

SEP - 2004

LOOKING FOR WAR

NOVELS BY DOUGLAS UNGER

Leaving the Land
El Yanqui
The Turkey War
Voices from Silence

LOOKING FOR WAR

and other stories

Douglas Unger

Ontario Review Press + Princeton, NJ

Ontario Review Press
9 Honey Brook Drive
Princeton, NJ 08540

Distributed by W. W. Norton & Co.
500 Fifth Avenue
New York, NY 10110

Library of Congress Cataloging-in-Publication Data

Unger, Douglas.
　　Looking for war / Douglas Unger.— 1st ed.
　　　p. cm.
　　Contents: Leslie and Sam—Tide pool—Cuban nights—The
perfect wife—The writer's widow—Autobiography—Matisse—
Looking for war.
　　ISBN 0-86538-111-9 (alk. paper)
　　　1. United States—Social life and customs—Fiction. I. Title.

PS3571.N45L66 2004
813'.54—dc22
　　　　　　　　　　　　　　　　　　　　　　　　　　　　2003063451
First Edition

Stories in this collection have appeared, in slightly different form, in
the following periodicals: "Leslie and Sam" in *Southwest Review*;
"Tide Pool" in *Ontario Review*; "The Perfect Wife," in *Colorado
Review*; "Cuban Nights" in *Idaho Review*; "The Writer's Widow" in
Ontario Review; "Autobiography" in *Iowa Review*; "Looking for War"
in *TriQuarterly*.

For Amy, dear wife, first reader, always,
in loving memory and still in dreams

CONTENTS

LOOKING FOR WAR

Leslie and Sam

They met in the Neurophysiology Lab. Carl and another new graduate student asked her to bring them one of the cats, a calico from a special breed with uniform dimensions of skulls and spines. They were on the research team doing a study on spinal cord regeneration. Carl invited her to stay and assist them—her first and only time assisting in surgery. A commanding way he had—as though there were never a question she would do what he asked—left her frustrated to the point of speechlessness. Some involuntary nervous response deep in her body started turning flips.

Masked and gowned as in an operating theater for humans, Leslie felt no squeamishness when Carl made his neat incision into the shaved skin patch in the fur of the anesthetized cat. She watched the pink and blue tissues dividing. She did her part—daubing with sterile gauze pads she gripped in forceps, soaking up the blood, impressed with how little bleeding there was and at Carl's deftly talented precision. But when he reached in with a tool like electrician's pliers and cut the exposed white spine—at the sickly crunching sound of living bone—she felt suddenly dizzy. There was a vague distant ringing in her ears. Then she was hovering in a hot sweat

1

somewhere out of her body, seeing everything as if looking down from inside the intense mirrored lights.

"Damnit! Did she say she was a greenhorn? Get her out of here and I'll keep the cat under!"

Carl's masked face was leaning down close to hers, his muffled voice shouting, the one clear strip of his features showing cold blue eyes that could have murdered. The other student helped Leslie slowly off the floor and held her up as she staggered out of the surgery room. She sat with her head between her knees until she recovered.

"You OK?" he asked, later. "Sorry to lose it in there. It was just a little delicate, what we were doing."

"So you get off on maiming small animals?"

"Subcortical mechanisms of behavior," he said. "I'll spend a lifetime cutting up cats. That is if I ever get the Ph.D. and make it through M-school, too. Which in my case is like a shoo-in, if you get what I mean."

He had found her in her supply room office just off the animal labs, where she could often be found studying or at the computer, sitting at the beat-up metal desk hidden away among the pallet loads of animal feeds rising up around her like heavy walls. He was in bloody green scrubs, looking her up and down with that predatory expression of the habitual ass-grabber. Leslie fixed him with her own most malicious answering stare and shrugged.

"Hey, I mean it," he said. "I'll buy you dinner."

That tone again. Why was she always falling for this kind of arrogant bastard? Why did so many women choose the wrong men? But that was the way it had started. As an ambitious M.D-Ph.D. student, Carl had a double schedule of classes and work in labs that would take up sixteen hours a day for six years before he was finished. Leslie wondered if he had just picked her out for convenience because she was so frequently in his path as he hurried from one place to another. He often slipped into her supply room office at any time as if just taking a break from his rushing around. They locked the door and spread out bags of monkey feed like a mattress. What bothered her the most was how she couldn't wait for the next of these flustered physical assaults on the job that came crashing into her serenity as would a carjacking. Then he snuck out like a thief and ran off on his rounds. But her girlfriends kept telling her what a catch he was. That she couldn't explain just how or why he had chosen her didn't change the fact that—outwardly and not knowing him better—Carl was the kind of guy most of them envied and desired.

The night he asked her to live with him, she arranged with her roommate for an evening to themselves. She cooked an elaborate, expensive dinner, a Salmon Joseph with wild rice and asparagus, to celebrate a difficult exam Carl had just finished taking in Biochemistry. He came in looking harried and exhausted, carrying a bottle of cheap brandy in a paper bag. Instead of sitting down to eat, he asked if he could fill her bathtub and take a bath first. As she was turning the burners down to warm and trying to save the fish from drying out, Carl pulled off his clothes, dropping them in a heap in the hallway. He carried his brandy into the bathroom and started filling the tub.

Minutes passed. Leslie heard the sound of his weeping, letting pain out in choking coughs he tried to swallow so no one could hear him. She ended up in the bathtub with him, holding him as he cried not with grief but from exhaustion. He had gotten an "A" on the exam and already knew he had. That was just the way he was—pretty much the way the whole relationship was going. Whatever he did, he did it all-out, full-time, non-stop, pushing himself to his limits until he finally broke down and collapsed into her arms. Then she was there to comfort him, mothering him, all further resistance she might have felt toward him melting away with his head leaning on her shoulder, rocking him in the tepid water until it went cold.

Eight months later, Leslie came in to work one Monday morning at the lab and saw the order regarding Sam, in Carl's handwriting and signed with his name. It was waiting for approval by Dr. Oxnard, sitting on top of a stack of forms in the lab office in-box. "Euthanize for cross-section sampling," the order said.

There wasn't any more reason or urgency to it than that. Kill Sam just to kill him, because there was nothing more important to do this week. Kill Sam because "it was just his time" as Dr. Oxnard said. Or because no one could dream up any more reasons to keep feeding him.

Leslie found Dr. Oxnard and offered to pay for Sam's feed. Dr. Oxnard said there was no way even to process such a contribution into the laboratory budget. She pleaded that she could take Sam home and keep him there. That was out because of public health regulations, the fact that rhesus monkeys were notorious carriers of human disease, especially tuberculosis, and keeping them outside the laboratory was against the health laws. No. The decision had been made.

"I'll miss him, too. Clever old fellow, really," Dr. Oxnard said with his Cambridge accent. "But he's an old man already, not much longer before he just keels over in his cage. We have plans to clear out all the old monkeys for the new neuroprotein study connected to Alzheimer's. NIH grant just came through. Big opportunity for the lab," he said. "I'm sorry, dear, really I am. Remember what I told you about forming close attachments to the study subjects?"

It was true that with Sam, Leslie had done things she shouldn't have, getting closer to him than she had realized. But he had just been so unusual. For the four years Leslie had been working in the lab thirty hours a week—the highest paying student job on campus—Sam had always been there. His first records file had been lost in a disastrous computer crash long ago and nobody even knew how old he was. His beard was gray. He was large for a rhesus monkey when he stretched himself up. But mostly, he sat hunched over like an arthritic old man in his cage, his yellow eyes showing the milky haze of cataracts, one of his dangerous canine fangs broken off, most of his other teeth worn to ugly brown stumps he showed when he yawned.

Sam had been used in so many experiments that he was useless for any more. Years ago, behavioral researchers had taught him a series of arrangements of colored plastic symbols—stars, circles, squares and triangles in red, blue and green they actually called a "language." Sam was strapped into a highchair and coached to arrange the symbols on his tray in a certain order to get a piece of banana, another to get a grape, another for an apple bit, and so forth, though whether rhesus monkeys could actually understand what they were doing with such symbols was still a controversy.

After that training, Sam was enrolled in drug addiction studies. Heroine. Cocaine. THC. Speed. Alcohol. They strung him out on almost everything. The Ph.D. candidates in Biopsychology were looking for data on behavioral changes based on Sam's manipulation of the plastic toys on the tray. When each study was completed, they left him in his cage to go cold turkey so another Ph.D. candidate could write down observations of his withdrawals.

Lab lore had it that Sam was addicted and detoxed this way to various substances more than twenty times. He was soon discovered to be an unreliable subject, and kept around and alive because he was. No matter what drugs he was given, whether he was high, stoned, drunk, cold sober, he was able to perform his games with the plastic symbols exactly the same way, perfectly and without variation. This innate tolerance or learned resistance—whatever it was—caused some excitement for a while then even further cycles of forced addiction until the researchers could be sure of what they observed. When they put him back in his cage for detoxing, Sam took even that as routine. Leslie had been there for the last two of these. Sam rolled up into the same fetal crouch, covered himself with his wood shavings, refused to eat for two weeks, and she observed he had even perfected a technique of turning his head carefully to one side so he could projectile vomit through the wire mesh and not soil his cage.

Like most monkeys in addiction studies, Sam probably would have been euthanized long ago to look at damage to his brain if he hadn't by lucky chance—or his own cleverness—one day gotten loose in the lab and been discovered by Dr. Oxnard at the supply room computer playing with a joystick. Sam was standing in the desk chair, intently staring at the monitor screen and rapidly pressing the trigger button on the stick as though he were actually playing a game called "Space Invasion."

"Never saw anything like it," Dr. Oxnard used to tell the story. "There he was, shooting down spaceships like he knew just what the game was about. But we never could get him to do it again. So he was probably just momentarily fascinated by the noise the damn thing was making."

The student who had held the job before Leslie had spent most of his time playing computer games in the supply room office. He was eventually fired for it, and for having such a lax attitude toward his duties in the Gross Anatomy lab upstairs. He was caught intentionally mixing up parts of carefully numbered cadavers and just tossing them into one big bag for incineration. He then divided up the pile of ashes into individual boxes as though it made no difference whose remains were finally returned to the families.

One of the reasons the job paid so well was to ensure a painstaking attitude toward the cadavers. Both that and to compensate for the revulsion most people felt at working so closely with dead bodies and what the first-year medical students did to them. Part of Leslie's job each day was to wheel a stainless steel cart through the Gross Anatomy lab that was like a forest of bluish-gray cadavers lying on the tables, rows of bodies with legs and arms often held up and spread out in metal stirrups as if in some final offertory ritual. When she was hired, Dr. Oxnard had given her his standard medical school pep talk about "the revered science of anatomy" and respect for what he called "the humanity of human remains."

Leslie had recognized the cadavers right away for their beauty and fascination. After all, they were still in some way people. They had had names and real lives, hopes and dreams, and she had never thought of the bodies on the tables as anything less. Her girlfriends asked her how she could do what she did without it giving her nightmares. But she was grateful to be working this job that paid enough she could almost painlessly support herself through college. Her father was a high school math teacher and her mother worked part-time for the school administration office in not too far off Winnetka. She and her sisters were made aware almost since they were capable of speech of the sharp irony that a high school teacher wouldn't have the money to send his kids to college. So she was proud of this job, what it meant for her and for her family. She did everything with care and responsibility. Each morning, before the medical students came to class, as Leslie slowly pushed her cart between the rows of steel tables, alone in a dense silence among the dead, eyes watering from the formaldehyde as she carefully, religiously emptied and kept track of the dissecting pans, she felt mainly a sense of peace.

Working with dead people was the easiest part of her job. After that, she took the elevator down to the basement, where she put on an apron and a pair of heavy rubber gloves. There were about a hundred rat cage trays to pull out and scrape off into a garbage can, fresh pellets in the food dishes, water bottles to wash out and fill, the rat cages rotating on a once-every-three-days schedule. Then there were the cats. The cats sometimes really did give her nightmares, the ones that were subjects in experiments and left alive that way, electrode ports sticking up out of their heads like bizarre metal horns, some with their brains cut up so radically they were blind and deaf and flopped over in twitching, cage-thumping seizures. The cats in Carl's spinal nerve regeneration studies were even more pathetic, a bank of cages filled mostly with black and orange calicos left miserably dragging their useless hindquarters around. She had to remind herself these cats served a noble purpose, research to help human paraplegics one day recover more of their lives. Only once every two days on a set schedule was she able to lift them out of their cages, limp helpless cats she raised up one after the other in a kind of sling as they meowed in pain or protest or just a kittenish demand for attention, she was never sure, then she cleaned out their cages and washed off their fur with a foul smelling antiseptic solution. After the cats—the cats that would break her heart if she allowed herself to think about them or even to stop for a moment to scratch one behind the ears—she moved her caretaking chores into the monkey room.

Sam would be waiting. It was only for Leslie or Dr. Oxnard that he stuck one black palmed hand out through the cage mesh, letting it dangle there as if a kind of greeting. She discovered through experimentation that what he wanted in the way of greeting was to grip one of her fingers tightly in his paw. After a minute or two, he would shake her finger twice and let it go. Then with Leslie—only with her, it seemed—he would leave his paw sticking out through the cage wire in a beckoning way. Leslie would put her much larger hand around his as Sam looked shyly away in his cage, even using his other hand like a kind of visor to shield his eyes. What he actually wanted was to hold hands, some form of intimate touch, she had no doubts. She would talk to him as they did this, asking him how his night had gone, then before she let go and continued with her chores, she always dropped some grapes or a piece of apple into his cage. Sam very slowly and not at all greedily let her hand go, collected his treats and turned his back to her, not wanting her to watch him eating.

There were twenty-six other monkeys in the room. They weren't at all like Sam as Leslie filled their biscuit racks and cleaned their cages. The other monkeys were often raucous, loud, screaming, "ook-ooking" as she called it, their paws gripping the wire mesh like so many little prisoners as they rattled and shook their cages all together with what seemed earthquake force. Then, suddenly, they settled down and sat watching her all in a troop with an oddly rustling kind of quiet and with what she felt was a fierce and primitive form of interspecies hatred.

Sam really was different from the others, she kept thinking. He was an escape artist, for one thing. The standard spring latch contraption on his cage door he had managed to open, reaching it with his paws by squeezing his arms through the wire mesh and bending them in an astonishing contortion. The lab had tried a padlock, but that had been a hassle because of always having to keep track of the key, and Sam kept up a constant slapping at the lock that made an incessant noise hard to stand. Then one night, he proved determined enough to chew through the cage wire, breaking off pieces of some of his teeth. Besides, the times he did get loose, undoing the wire latch and just lifting up his sliding cage door, all he ever really did was wander around looking for bits of spilled biscuits from the other cages. Every once in a while, Leslie found him sitting in front of one of the female monkey's cages, both reaching out their paws, grooming each other, or using the hairy back of a paw to stroke each other's cheeks—Dr. Oxnard once told her whimsically that was the way monkeys kissed.

When Leslie found Sam loose in the monkey room—or even the times she had opened the door to her supply room office and let him come in and join her while she was studying—whenever Sam was loose for long enough, as though he were finished with what he wanted to do outside, he lazily stretched and yawned then crept off on all fours back into the monkey room where he would let himself back inside his cage, sliding his door closed behind him.

A monkey goes in search of its cage. What did that mean? Leslie often wondered. And thinking about Sam now—desperate fantasies of setting him free—she knew that even if she could just lead him out of the laboratory into the elevator and set him loose into the grass and trees of the hospital campus, or even if she could get him into a taxi and take him farther than that, out of the city to some large park or wild stretch of rivers and woods, no matter what Leslie could imagine doing, she knew that, in the end, since his birth knowing no other world, Sam was smart enough that he would eventually find his own way back like a lost dog returning home.

"What? You're kidding! That smelly old thing?"

This was Carl's reaction to her pleas to save Sam.

"Come on. Don't go anti-vivisectionist on me. We've got enough trouble with those freaks. Leslie, please," he said when it was clear she would only answer him with an enraged silence. "Don't be like this. You know the reality of what we're doing."

Finally, she told herself it wasn't Carl, that he wasn't in any way to blame—he was just the one there for the job. Still, the night she found out, she was upset enough that she found his bottle of sleeping pills he rarely used and took two to calm herself down. Later, in bed, she felt her skin flinching when Carl pulled her to him—how strong he was, the way he could just lift her around in bed as helpless as a monkey pinned by its arms. She lifelessly let him screw her while she pushed her fogging mind somewhere else.

"Don't be like this," Carl pleaded, softly.

She didn't answer. She turned her back to him. As she was slowly drifting into a drugged sleep, she sensed one of his strong competent hands gently feeling along the bones of her spine.

The next morning, the note Carl left stuck with a magnet to the refrigerator said only, *You've been avoiding me. We need to talk—C.*

She picked up his socks. She had never had a relationship with a man who didn't leave his socks on the floor. She gathered up his shirts, underwear and surgical greens piled on a chair. Collecting the laundry was part of her routine. For the past eight months, she had ended up doing his wash, the shopping, cooking what meals they shared increasingly mindful that he was probably only with her for the comforts she provided him. Carl could have any number of attractive girls. Nurses and technicians at the hospital were always throwing themselves at him. More and more, she felt an ache like a premonition of the deep hurt she would feel when he finally left her for one of them.

And now there was this problem over Sam. She realized she felt about Sam almost the same confused emotions she was feeling for Carl—how she looked at him now like he was already gone. How was it possible to go on living this way? Her own plans had very slowly and subtly changed, as though submerged into the daily patterns of this routine of life with him. She had once imagined she would receive her college degree then go on to graduate school in a field of environmental science—youthful visions she had conceived since high school of one day helping to preserve forests, riparian habitats, vanishing species. How had she managed to let most of this senior year go by without even applying? All of it came down to him—him, him, him, she realized. As she went out that morning into the grimy winter light of Chicago, she looked around their small shabby apartment with an awareness like a stab at the center of her being that everything would soon be a memory.

Sam. She went right to him, first thing, letting go her chores in the Gross Anatomy lab upstairs. There he was, waiting, his hand poking out through the wire mesh in that way he had. She let him grip her finger a long time, then she opened up his cage door and set a handful of grapes down in his wood shavings. Sam looked at the abundance of them a little warily. He slowly collected the grapes, one by one, like he was counting them, moving them around with his gnarled old paws, his wrists scarred like a suicide survivor's with multiple cuts, needle marks, slashes from so many times he had been hooked up to machines. He held a grape up to his nose and sniffed it then turned his back on her and ate it, as was his custom, as if too shy to let anyone see him eating.

Sam turned and faced her again. So unlike the other monkeys who took direct eye contact as a challenge, Sam could look any human being straight in the eyes as if fixing that person in his mind with his sharp yellow gaze. He did this to Leslie now. He curled his lip at her, a sign he wanted to play. He actually gestured with two fingers at his grapes, then he began arranging them in a star shape in the shavings.

"Not hungry?" she asked.

He looked at her again in that deep way. He arranged his grapes into a square and fixed on her again.

"Apple?" she asked. She pulled one from her lab coat pocket and held it out. He took the apple quickly, turned his back, and she watched the shifting, hunched-over movements as he greedily ate the whole thing. "Good for you, Sam. Good for you," she said.

She picked up her book. She had discovered on one of Sam's afternoons in the supply room office with her that he liked to hear her read. She had been reading sentences from one of her term papers off the computer screen to make sure of the rhythms and she had glanced over at Sam, finding him actually listening, his head cocked a little to one side, then as she kept on reading, she watched what looked like a pleased and tranquil mood come over him, his gray beard even nodding to the rhythm of her words as if to some gentle music. She experimented with this. Whenever she stopped reading, she noticed that Sam sat up and started shifting impatiently around, sniffing and poking his fingers at the bags of feed. Then when she started reading again aloud, he quit that and settled down, leaning back with what she thought was a pleasant, dreamy expression.

His apple finished, she watched as Sam turned again, facing her. He reached out through the open cage door with his paw as though waiting for her to let him grab and squeeze her finger all over again.

"No," she said. "I'll read to you now."

She was a senior, and like many Biology students, she had put off her core requirements in the Humanities as long as she could. The class was working its way through a *Masterpieces of World Literature: Volume One* anthology this semester. She opened the thick expensive book to the assignment for today and started reading: "Betwixt mine eye and heart a league is took / And each doth good turns now unto the other: / When that mine eye is famish'd for a look / Or heart in love with sighs himself doth smother / With my love's picture then my eye doth feast / And to the painted banquet bids my heart..."

It was the wrong thing to read. She couldn't go on. All she could do was keep repeating, though she wasn't sure the sounds she was making actually formed words, "I'm sorry, Sam... I'm sorry... I'm so sorry... I'm sorry... I'm sorry..."

She saw her future. Tomorrow, coming into the monkey room and finding Sam's cage empty. Then she saw the life ahead of her with Carl—how she would become even more attached, allied with him, cooking his meals, cleaning his place, picking up his socks and shirts. How he would pull her to him in the night and use her whenever he needed. And she would give him all he wanted, everything, see to all his comforts, see him through medical school, gladly, devotedly, more and more, until the day would come when his ambitious dreams were all she had left to call her own.

Sure, they might even get married—she was woman enough to keep him tied to the comforts she provided him so he would feel obliged to marry her and he would. He would get his degrees and make six figures in income. They would drive new cars and move into a beautiful house. She would put the house together for him, make his home her world. She would have his children. For a time, she would even be happy. But all the while, she would be waiting for a day like this one, the day Carl didn't come home, the day some nurse or lab-tech caught his eye on his hurrying way from one place to another and what she always sensed would happen would finally happen and that would be the end.

She would be alone, and, sure, missing the feel of his always rushing body, his delicate surgeon's touch, longing for his companionship and self-assured voice, the strong vanilla and medicine smell of him that was uniquely his no matter where he had been. Then she would be lost. Why it would never work out was the way she had already lost herself and would keep losing herself in him, dissolving into him like into some unstable absorbent solution until there was nothing left of herself, nothing of her own she could even recognize. That was it—she was already lost, and she knew this now, knew it as surely and certainly as she had ever known anything in her life.

No. Better to be alone now than let herself be destroyed by what was surely coming. And this job—she had worked it too long, she knew that much now, too. Once they killed Sam, she could never, ever set foot in this lab again. She would finish reading to him, yes, she would, read to him until he fell asleep or turned away in his cage. She would say her last good-bye then go to the supply room office to type up a letter of resignation to put on Dr. Oxnard's desk. From there, she would go directly home. She would pull out the empty boxes, suitcases and plastic bags and start packing. She would be gone to a friend's house before Carl turned up for dinner. She would leave a note for him on the refrigerator: *Let's not talk after all. I've decided to avoid you for the rest of my life.—L.*

Leslie sat there thinking all of this, seeing pictures in her mind in fast jumping images like a series of shaky disconnected scenes searching forward on a video. And now she was pushing the rewind button before the scenes ever had the chance to happen. She became suddenly aware of herself. Her eyes were closed, her body bent over and leaning against Sam's cage, her arms wrapped tightly around her middle as if to catch herself from the sensation she was falling. She was crying, making painful human sounds.

Suddenly, she stiffened. A sob caught still in her throat when she realized what it was, on the side of her face, such a light hairy sensation it almost tickled. Years later, she would describe what happened as one of the most tender and loving touches she ever experienced—how a monkey had once kissed her that way on the cheek.

Tide Pool

Almost everything about their second honeymoon would be clean and white—the sandy shores of the island, the hotel, the crisp cotton clothes they would wear, even the strong local rum was white. White was just perfect. She was seeking spiritual renewal, reaffirming their love, rebuilding their dreams.

A physicist acquaintance from Wisconsin, John, and his wife, Merle, often traveled to an island off the coast of Brazil. They suggested that George and Sally join them. Sally read up about the place—what seemed a paradise in the deep blue bay of Bahia de Todos os Santos called Itaparica. Lush tropical forests covered the island. All around were picturesque white sand and rocky beaches. The great blue whales from all over the Atlantic gathered once a year mysteriously to court each other in the bay, rolling and spouting in the waves, then they mated and swam off to sea. Just a short boat ride away was the eccentric and mythical city of Bahia—called the Black Rome of Brazil—with its African-Brazilian culture, food, music, and its benign voodoo-like ceremonies called Candomblé, promising a city where people could be seen at all hours literally dancing in the streets.

While Sally leafed through the books filled with glossy photos of palm-shaded turquoise visions of where they would be—*I-ta-pa-ri-ca*, she kept sounding out the word like an incantation—her daydreams of such a romantic wild place made her realize how long she had been deprived. The feeling was like waking up startled after lying in the sun too long—that sudden dreaded discomfort of the burn. Her marriage had become all about George in its first seven years, his struggles and frustrations, his endless days and nights finishing the research and writing for a Ph.D. in Physics. His dissertation on high energy particle beam theory—a thin bound volume of graphs, charts and hieroglyphic calculations that filled her with an anxiety close to terror every time she saw the dense strange numbers and letters in Greek—had taken up most of the last four years. She worked as a legal assistant, her own days caught up in the arcane, complex language of contracts and the law. But even with her experience of obscure, convoluted statements, she still felt remote, foolish even, when she tried to decipher the technical jargon of science and abstraction which she dutifully typed for George to meet his deadlines.

Once or twice a week, they made quick love in between George's appointments with supercomputers and datalinks and trips to the particle accelerator in Illinois. Whatever else they did together as a couple seemed hard for her even to remember—mindless hours with their feet up in front of the television, low budget dinner parties at the homes of other graduate students when they all drank too much cheap wine and laughed at conversations they couldn't recall the next morning. Some weekends, they went on drives up through the mountains and trees and glaciers. She took the wheel while George stared out the window not really seeing anything through his spaced-out distractions. She understood that was a normal state of mind for most physicists—she had been told the story that, after World War Two, when government authorities finally granted the security clearance, having denied it to him for years for his pacifism, Albert Einstein required an army corporal assigned to him at Los Alamos because he kept forgetting how to get to the men's room and mess hall and barracks. She concluded that physicists were by nature distracted types. With George, she suffered from an increasing sense that she was experiencing the world completely alone. She couldn't imagine whatever it was they were living was any kind of life. For all those years, it was she who mainly supported them, cooked their meals, kept up their small and far too expensive apartment in Boulder, Colorado, with its view out the kitchen window to the almost black mountains like jagged looming slabs of wrought iron standing guard over the high-tech city.

Finally, she watched George hooded as he received his degree, published his papers, then landed a job with a more than adequate salary at the nearby Lockheed-Martin research institute outside of Denver—a position partly funded by NASA, in part by the Department of Defense. So life promised change now. They decided to gamble everything they had saved on this one long trip before he started his new job—this second honeymoon, as George jokingly called it, though she had never thought of it just that way—this chance to recover their lives. She was just at that point when she felt she had lost all vision of what it was she really wanted. She needed to talk this over with him but only under the right conditions, somewhere else—*Ita-pa-ri-ca*—this place where she hoped they both could open themselves to new personal discoveries. As she planned the trip and daydreamed of the possibilities—

not only for herself but for him, too, for them both—she grew steadily more aware of how resentful of their life she had become. And resentment was like a black spider spinning away inside their love.

The resort hotel John and Merle booked for them was a Portuguese colonial building with a classical look made of white stone, surrounded by white columns and enclosing a beautiful white marble courtyard. It was everything she had wished for—rustic hemp hammocks under banana trees, lunch and drinks delivered poolside, perches and branches full of huge red, green, and blue colored birds singing and screeching to them overhead. Even John and Merle were discreet, leaving them on their own but for an occasional lunch or dinner or excursion on the island. For the first time, she had the sense that all that lay before her—everything she could reach out and grasp and call her life—fulfilled what she had dreamed.

They had lunch with John and Merle in the village square amid the thrill of their arrival, laughing and joking as they sat together at one of the wrought-iron patio tables set out under the trees. John explained how each tall, broad-leafed, tropical tree with silvery white trunk set around the plaza had an individual name given to it by the villagers. The common belief on the island was that the trees had living souls, magical powers for either good or evil or anything in between, spirits that lived inside them. African and Catholic religions had combined here—saints from Rome went hand in hand with forest and sea gods from African Candomblé rituals—and even the ground under their feet, the tiles of the plaza, each stone in the paved pathways, each sprig of grass and coconut on the beach, everything on the island was considered either blessed or cursed by the saints and gods.

"Everything on Itaparica is alive," John said. "You'll see. A most magical and inspired place," he said. "And the natives here believe some things and some people have been alive among us more than once. Look at that strange fellow over there." John pointed out a small, brown and pitifully thin, unshaven man, barefoot, the filthy clothes hanging on his body barely dignified enough to call them rags. On his head was a billed blue naval officer's cap cocked to one side. "That man thinks he's the reincarnation of a seventeenth-century Dutch sea captain who lost his life in a battle with the Portuguese. Even though he was born on the island and has hardly left it even to go across the bay to Bahia, no one on Itaparica would think of disagreeing with him. They give him food, spare change, buy him drinks and call him very respectfully Capitán."

The odd little man eventually came around to their table and showed off a gap-toothed grin. He held out his dirty hand in a demanding way. Sally shrank back from him, reeling from his strong sour smell and the way he was scratching himself with his other hand, her thought that he might get close enough she could catch something. But George dug into his pockets and gave the little man some colorful bills of Brazilian money. He delighted in ordering him a large bottle of beer, saluting him and calling him Capitán. The little sea captain saluted back, eyes glittering, spouting what seemed to be senseless strings of disconnected sounding phrases in a language John assured everyone was, amazingly, an authentic seventeenth-century Dutch dialect no one had any idea how he might have learned.

From what Sally could see, the man was obviously schizophrenic and insane. She watched him work his way around to the other tables with his chin high, his chest thrust out, everything about him carrying an air of official dignity. Their lunch came, an oyster casserole called a *muceca* followed by platters of deep fried fish, potatoes, vegetables, and more rounds of beer. By the time they were through the meal they were laughing again, happily speculating about just what it would take for them to toss all pretense of their busy former worlds aside. They would build shacks on the beach and become contented tranquil bums on Itaparica for the rest of their lives. "Or the way they look at it here, who knows for how many additional lives worth of reincarnations," John said.

Later, John and Merle left them to take a nap. Sally walked off the beer and heavy meal on the beach with George, listening to the birds, gazing out into the deep blue bay at the whale spouts and white breakers where the huge beasts were rolling and splashing and slapping their tails in the distance. She felt something strange about him—an extra tension in his arm as he offered it to her when they walked, a certain hardness about his face, and within him a deeper silence, if that were possible.

That night, in the moonlit darkness under the rhythmic whipping blade of the ceiling fan, they made love in a drugged hazy intensity effected by too many local raw rum and lime juice drinks called *caipirinhas*. He took her roughly, strongly— so unlike any other time she could remember. She had always seen herself in charge in that way. Here, there was something strange and powerful, even brutal in him. She had trouble breathing in the wet tropical heat. She was startled, scared, as if her heart might suddenly stop. She closed her eyes. The hair on his body felt rough and scratchy like an old matted rug. She resisted a little but he pinned her down. He moved on her with a power she had never before sensed in him until he broke the night with his shouts.

This wasn't quite the renewal she had expected. She had long ago resigned herself to the physical nature of her husband as a thin, gaunt, pasty white body too long locked up and atrophied in the confinement of laboratories with chalkboards and computer screens. Sometimes, at home, she imagined as they made love that he was actually working calculations in his head. Usually, it was she who initiated everything regarding sex—she had complained just once about this to her sister and Anne had gone so far as calling him a wimp. OK, at least George had always been a gentle and lovable guy, even if he was a bit wimpy and withdrawn. But here, on this island, something happened to him overnight. It was as if he turned brown under the strong sun in a single day. His physical size seemed to grow. She felt muscles on his body she had never felt or noticed before. When he took off his thick glasses while undressing in the room, she was shocked by how different even his face looked now—as if she had somehow formed a picture of him in her mind of studious George, dedicated George, reliably quiet George to the point where she had begun never to see him as anything else. Now, when she tried to settle down to talk with him in the evenings in their beautiful white room overlooking the gentle waves on the moonlit bay—these serious talks she had been anticipating for weeks about what they were going to do to change, to reclaim their lives—he shushed her quickly. He all but ripped the white cotton nightgown off her body and took her roughly in his arms.

She woke up early in the morning feeling strange— confused but not unhappy. No, she reflected over strong Brazilian coffee, she was not at all unhappy at this change in him. What she felt was something on the borderline of being frightened—and it wasn't unpleasant really to find herself just short of being actually scared. This fear came in sudden and unexpected starts, instinctive, like a reflex reaction to the noise of a door loudly banging shut or something crashing in the night. And what of all the things she had planned to say? She had gone over and over the words in her mind for so many weeks, the way she had seen attorneys rehearsing closing arguments. She had to get across to him how they had to find a different way to live, something deeper and steadier in the way of communication. She had even thought of counseling to help them find the things to do together to feed their spirits, their togetherness, their married life.

Sally tried to talk about what was bothering her to Merle one morning when they were walking together along one of the rockier beaches of the island. She found that all she had thought about saying, somehow, she was no longer able to put into words exactly now even for herself, as though the effect of the island, or of the tropical heat and humidity, had caused a hot misting confusion to fall across her thinking. It seemed to her she was walking around all day on this island in a foggy half sleep like she had just awakened from a nap. John and George were off looking at the dismantling of some kind of NATO defense facility—for years, there were underwater sonar buoys placed all over the bay of Bahia dedicated to long-distance listening for enemy submarines, the geography and shape of the bay like a large open ear turned toward the whole Atlantic. John's field of specialty was ultra-low frequency sound. Both had donned short-sleeved white shirts and ties, security IDs clipped to their pockets. So, even here they were working.

Sally and Merle strolled along the beach between the fringe of the dark green treeline and the turquoise water. Colorful birds squawked and wheeled around overhead.

Catlike mongooses—imported a generation ago from India to control snakes on the island—rustled and scurried in the undergrowth. Sally walked on the beach with a deep, almost mystical sense of their own smallness at the edge of the sea. She tried her best to explain to Merle what she was feeling and her husband's strange and somehow frightening change.

"Oh, yes, well...I guess there's a reason John and I keep coming back to Itaparica year after year," Merle said. She smiled quickly and flushed a little. "John becomes positively like a teenager every time. Amazing, really. And I can't say I mind at all..."

"No. That's...great," Sally said. "It's just that George is so... so *different*. It's hard even to talk about the future, how it's going to be when we get back to our lives."

"But this *is* your life, isn't it?" Merle asked. "I mean, isn't what happens here, the way it is now, really the way you want it to be?"

"Yes...Yes, and no," Sally said. "I mean," she waved an arm helplessly at the sea in a sweeping gesture, frustrated, like tossing something away. "I just can't think of all of this as real," she said.

"But this *is* real," Merle said. "This island is more real than anywhere else on earth. I mean, you've seen the whales. They must know something. Why do you think they keep coming to this beautiful bay year after year since the beginning of time?"

"I'm not complaining. Please don't misunderstand," Sally said. "It's just that I had hoped actually to talk, to make plans, commitments, to discuss just what it is we're really doing...."

"Oh, well then, please," Merle said. "This isn't the place for that kind of thing. You don't come to Itaparica to talk about things like that. Just enjoy the time here, the effect it has on you both. Look! Look around! Live a little, right now, for a change. Forget any serious things until you get back home. If you ask me, the trouble with most marriages is there's far too much serious talk. The minute a man and woman fall in love and get married, they should quit all serious talks. Men hate serious talks. And all serious talks ever got most women is a sour disposition and more wrinkles on her face."

Suddenly, they came upon a small cove, carved out among the overhanging trees. Waves broke against coral outcroppings and rounded stones. It was just after low tide. Like large shining jewels scattered in the white sand were the most beautiful and unusual looking shells. Merle pointed them out with a little girlish sound of delight—conch shells in a lilac color, tiger-striped conical shells, pink and blue spotted shells, serrated clam-shaped shells the size of her hand and that glowed with a spectral, almost unearthly orange and emerald green. Merle started gathering an armful of the pretty shells. Sally followed, her thoughts of George, of their lives together and her vague foreboding of discontentment to come, all of this was suddenly lifted from her as if by the miraculous sight of these shells set like gemstones in the white sand.

Sally carefully picked over the shells in the cove. She watched each one a moment, waiting for some inner sense that it was the right one, as if the shell could somehow speak to her, saying something real she needed to know. In this way, gradually, bent over and searching through the sand, rocks and pool, she collected a black and orange leopard spotted shell, a conch like a glowing blue violet, two each of pink and orange and turquoise colors, and one which was as big as both her fists put together that was the most beautiful translucent white like the finest porcelain. They spent the rest of the morning gathering shells in the shade of the overhanging trees, the blue water breaking into salt white foam at their feet as the tide began coming in. She couldn't imagine or remember more beautiful and peaceful hours in her life.

After dinner that night, George couldn't even wait until dessert. He literally picked her up from the seaview patio where they were dining. She was shocked at how light she felt in his arms, how little she seemed made of as he carried her to their room. He tossed her on the bed and rifled the clothes off her body. Somehow, he forced her, finally, to let go. She lay back and looked up at the ceiling fan beating the air over them, her arms spread, her fists gripping handfuls of the sheets. He made love to her that way what seemed most of the night. Their voices rose and fell then rose again together in passionate, singing screams.

Her illness started the day after they returned home. Before bed, she had hastily unpacked, tossing her beach clothes and white cotton tropical dresses into the laundry basket, haphazardly taking her collection of colorful seashells out of their plastic bag and making a quick arrangement of them on her bedside table.

The next morning, she awoke feeling loggy and short of breath. There was a terrible stinging pain at the side of her neck. It was difficult to move. She thought she must be suffering a reaction from traveling—some minor bug she might have picked up from the spicy food. She apologized to George that she couldn't get out of bed. He tenderly kissed her. She watched as he dressed, distractedly hunted up his pocket protector and his keys then went off to his first day at his new job.

She lay in bed and dozed but the pain got worse. By three o'clock in the afternoon, her joints were stiff, her limbs so numb that she became alarmed. She tried to get out of bed and discovered she couldn't walk. She had to drag herself across the floor to the bathroom. It was an agony to lift her body up by the edge of the sink. When she looked in the mirror, she let out a stifled shout at what she saw—her features gone slack, her face a blur from eyes unable to focus, involuntarily shifting back and forth, side to side in her head. She heard a loud ringing in her ears then sank to the floor with a moan.

She came to enough to drag herself to the telephone and dial 911. There was a daze of the paramedics breaking open the front door, vague sensations of her body lifted onto the wheeled stretcher and carried out, then blackness. When she woke up in the hospital, she had a tube stuck down her throat connected to a ventilator, other tubes sprouting from her arms. She was surrounded by pulsing beeping machinery and a blur of masked alien faces, doctors and nurses in plastic suits looking down at her. She heard distant scattered words, *Toxic response. Epinephrine. Dehydration. Isolation. Disease of unknown origins...*

Later, she awoke feeling better. At least she could bend and unbend her elbows and knees. Then she saw George pacing back and forth at the foot of the bed, shoulders slumped over, a startled, terrified look on his face. She tried to say something—impossible with the tube down her throat—but her stirring caused him to turn and see her watching him. He jumped to her side, holding her hand, kissing her as though she had been somehow saved. She made motions at her throat—God but the tube was uncomfortable—and gestured for help with it. She felt she was all right now. She was strong enough in her chest she could almost fight back the rhythmic mechanical pumping and sucking of air driven forcibly into her lungs.

The tube was taken out that evening. She breathed comfortably on her own. She felt clear-headed, just fine, even hungry. "What the hell happened?" she asked George. "What do the doctors say?"

"Don't worry about that. Whatever it was, it's over now. What a scare," he said.

"What do they say was wrong?"

"They don't know. They did every test in the book. There's no disease. Some kind of reaction. One of them even asked if you were allergic to strawberries or had been stung by a bee, of all things."

She looked out the hospital window at a cold blowing snow against the black slabs of mountains. "Bees? Are they crazy?"

"I'm just so grateful you're back," he said. Then he knelt down and buried his face in her blankets, his thick glasses flopping off one ear like a busted swing. He was crying. It was hard for her to reach her hand out because of the IV tubes. Still, she managed to stroke his head. Poor George. Poor helpless George, she thought. She pulled her hand away, feeling strangely removed, distant, cold. This was the husband she knew. This was really coming home.

She was released from the hospital in two days, feeling drained but well enough finally to unpack, do the laundry from their trip, get organized. She hung up on her kitchen walls the pictures she had bought at a Bahia street fair of black Brazilian women huddled over teapots and with turbans around their heads. She draped the good luck ribbons they had bought from a little girl on the steps of the Nostro Senhor do Bonfim cathedral around the bedroom windows. On impulse, she went out and bought lengths of fabric in yellow, green and blue—the colors of Brazil—then she arranged them in a decorative drapery in one corner of the living room. She didn't want to do much more, looking around at their small inadequate apartment and knowing, with George's success at his new job, they would be moving soon.

Her seashells she kept in the bedroom. She liked them on the night table beside the bed. Sometimes, she lay back in bed and held one up, staring into its leopard spots or iridescent colors, holding the white one up and looking through it directly into the light—she found a dark shadow deep inside that fascinated her—then she vividly recalled the wild nights they had lived on Itaparica. She sniffed at the shells to recapture the salt sea smell, held them to her ears to listen, something in the sound making her hear again the high-pitched calls of the toucans and parrots, see again all the colorful birds.

She called in sick again to her job that next week. Her focus was on George. He came home with a briefcase full of computer sheets and thick binders full of data to go over each night in preparation for the next day. But he was happy. She could see that. She watched him work at the kitchen table messy with papers where he had always worked. She came up behind him from time to time, encircled him with her arms and kissed his head. Finally, he stirred. He followed her—maybe a bit tired, a bit reluctantly—into the bedroom.

Sunday morning, her illness set in again. George woke up to her weakly flailing arms going numb, just then losing all sensation. Sally was making a pitiful whistling sound, all she could do trying to call out. Her eyes—how they shifted, darted side to side in her head with such an expression of fear. He threw back the covers, rushed to the telephone. In the ambulance, on the way to the hospital, her heart stopped. The paramedics used the paddles to shock her back to life.

The specialist in contagious diseases called in, a Dr. Feingold, from Denver, looked in at her through a window with him from the hallway just outside Intensive Care. There she was, drugged and sleeping, breathing with the pump and whoosh of a ventilator, IV needles trailing tubes. There was something strange and noncommittal in the doctor's manner, George thought, and in the way he kept raising his fingers up to his lips and chin, rubbing them like a guy who hasn't shaved in two days compulsively scrapes the stubble on his face.

"Can't you tell us *any*thing?" George asked.

"To be honest, we don't have a clue," Dr. Feingold said. "But I've heard of cases like this, from Africa, and it's on her chart that you just got back from a trip to Brazil. Did she eat any strange food, like an unusual fish? Do you remember her getting bitten by anything?"

"We ate just...*food*...what everybody eats there. Sure. Fish, oysters in casserole, lots of seafood and rice and that saw-dust stuff they call *farofa*, plenty of that. But no bites from anything. There were hardly even any mosquitoes. Are you saying it might be something she ate?"

"It's sure something," Dr. Feingold said. "We should do more tests. My guess is it's a reaction to something from there."

This time, George decided to celebrate her recovery and homecoming with a cookout. No matter if it was winter, in Boulder, the sun still broke through whatever weather there was most days, a high bright mountain sun that shone over the black flatiron peaks and turned the world into a sparkling blue brilliance from the melting ice and snow. And Sally had always loved it when they barbecued, her turn to let him cook, using the cheap little grill on the courtyard lawn of the apartment complex. The fresh air might do her good, he thought. She could sit at the picnic table in her sunglasses and they could gaze up together—the way she liked—at the evergreens on the table mesa and the dark striking mountains against the sky.

But she didn't look good to him, not good at all, and he started to worry that she should be outside. She had lost weight. Her face was thin now, gaunt, the skin sagging in places. Getting her in or out of the ambulance, something had cut her cheek, and she still wore a patch of iodine-yellowed gauze. There were deep bluish circles under her eyes. She reached out a hand that looked like a pack of loose bones in a translucent coin purse, skin splotched black and blue from needle marks, her fingers trembling as she lifted a wine glass—wine was OK if she could keep it to just one glass. He watched her raising the wine to her dry, cracked lips.

George tried to be as cheerful as he could be as he waved away the charcoal smoke and turned the lamb chops on the grill. He found himself rattling on about his new job—the speculative math of subatomic particle theory, an aberration in old nuclear testing data he had discovered, and a model he was designing that might one day uncover at least one small bit of the most incomprehensible secrets of the cosmos, concepts classically judged not only by their accuracy as equations but also in such aesthetic terms as *symmetry, harmony, beauty*—he felt he and his colleagues were sounding more and more like soppy romantic poets whenever they discussed their theories. As he talked on, he observed her, cautiously, trying not to show his concern as she started shivering even though she was bundled up in two sweaters and a goose-down winter coat. "This was a bad idea," he said. "It's just too damned cold. Let's move it indoors, Sweetheart, where you can be more comfortable."

"No. I'm just fine out here. It was a wonderful idea. This is just what I mean," she said. "Doing things like this. Simple things. Just like this," she said. Even with her sunglasses on, he could see a dazed, distant expression in her eyes which startled him. He was about to insist more firmly that they move indoors as soon as the chops were off the grill. "Oh look!" she said suddenly. "Over there! Look! *That's* so beautiful!"

He turned his head in the direction she was pointing and saw them—a doe and her fawn, almost fully grown, had bounded over the apartment complex hedge and were walking slowly, unbothered and unafraid, across the patches of melting snow on the far side of the lawn. Their gray-brown coats were long and fluffed up and shone in the sun. The doe turned and nudged the younger one along, then they both shook their long mule ears and jumped easily over the far hedge into a neighboring yard.

"Right here," Sally said. "Right in town like this. That's something. This really is a beautiful place to live," she said again, then her voice cracked. "Oh, God, God, George, what's *wrong* with me," she sobbed.

She let her head fall into her arms and started to cry so hard that he pulled the chops off the grill half-cooked. Saying how sorry he was, it was too much, much too much to expect her first day home, he lifted her, still weeping, and carried her across the lawn and through the sliding glass doors of their apartment. He put her straight to bed, undressing her like a huge limp doll. He helped her into pajamas, pulled the covers over her and tucked her in. When he tried to serve her dinner in bed, she said she wasn't hungry. Her voice sounded strangely thin, far away. All she wanted to do was lie back weakly on her pillow, holding her big white conch shell up to the window, staring through it into the light.

He stayed home from work for the next three days to take care of her, bringing her soups she hardly touched, cups of tea she held in her hands for warmth until they went cold. She slept most of the time, writhing and moaning in her dreams, her eyes blinking open suddenly when she woke up with a shout. He calmed her and stroked her forehead, which felt alarmingly cool. He called Dr. Feingold's office several times. The most the doctor told him to do when he finally did return the messages was to check if she were breathing clearly and see if there were any swelling anywhere. She was probably just tired out and still recovering. They had an appointment at Dr. Feingold's office on Friday. He seemed to think that was soon enough.

George hung up the phone and went in to check on Sally again, as he was doing now every few minutes. He paced back and forth at the foot of the bed, wondering what it was, what had happened, and feeling weirdly haunted by the thought that it was all somehow caused by him. How strange he had acted in Brazil! How unlike himself! What the hell had happened to him! He searched his memory, every move, every day, over and over again, reviewing all they had done to the minutest details—what full lives they had lived there, what, astonishing intimacy, he realized, with infinite variations each moment he recalled. He made lists of food, insects they had seen, people they had touched. He came up with nothing that could explain it. In conclusion, he couldn't shake off the repeated irrational conviction that whatever was wrong with her had something to do with him.

He shuddered at the thought of the way he had been, promising himself that if they could get through all of this, he would make it up to her. He would go easier at his job. He would find the time she wanted him to take to devote to them. He would do anything and everything she wanted—once he really knew just what that was—and, in wondering about this, he lost himself for hours again in the possibilities like working through a complex formula with multiple solutions. Full of a deep and yet pitifully sad love for his sick wife, he finally crawled into the bed beside her, exhausted, and held her as calmingly as he could through her fitful dreams.

Thursday night, it happened again. He felt her getting sick soon after the attack started, her weakness, and those darting, uncontrollable eyes. He leapt out of bed to call the ambulance. Still, as quick as he had reacted, before the paramedics came, every breath she took was a hoarse rattling, and she made a terrible moaning sound. He felt her breathing shutting down. He held her head and tried to blow air through her lips and down her windpipe. Her last look at him before her eyes rolled white in her head was all helplessness and panic—the look of someone drowning. "Hold on, hold on," was all he could say. Then with a sick premonition she might never hear him again, he shouted, "I love you! I love you!"

She died that night. They had managed to get the tube down her throat again. She was just hooked up, given strong injections and being monitored in Intensive Care when her heart just suddenly stopped. They spent more than an hour trying to shock her back alive. Dr. Feingold couldn't be reached. The resident in charge made the call. He stood in the hallway with George, the young doctor baffled, just staring at the floor, shaking his head. George started shouting at him and at the nurses. He pounded his fists on the walls. He cried out at them with strings of threats about lawsuits, incompetence, malpractice. How could something like this happen? Who the hell had been in charge? A team of security guards finally surrounded him in the hallway and forced him to leave the building.

After all of that, in the parking lot, he realized he hadn't even asked to be let in to see her dead. But what good would that do? He knew it wouldn't be her anymore he would have seen.

He went home to their apartment. He cried all night. At times, he beat the couch cushions, then the walls. He tore at his hair in a grief-stricken rage. By morning, he had barely enough hold on himself to start making calls. Her mother, first. Then her sister. Then her boss and some of her friends. He found himself listening to a dull monotonic voice he could hardly recognize as his own. He didn't say much to any of them—an illness she had, nobody knew what it was, had killed her, will call again when he made arrangements. In all of this, as he understood was the case with a death so sudden and unexplained, he sensed people listening to his incomplete and unsatisfactory words might somehow be blaming him.

At one point, he just couldn't take it anymore. He leapt up and started punching his head with his fists. He threw himself into walls and around the room. Then he collapsed again on the couch crying out why, why, why. It wasn't fair. It struck him just how near they had come, somewhere on that island, to a closeness like a mystery she had been seeking all along, and that he only realized now, when it was too late. And he felt that he had failed her, that they should never have left, should have said damn and to hell with it all and never come home. What was it worth now? What was any of it really worth? The strange tragic conviction that it was somehow he who had really caused her death—the way he had become on the island or what he could no longer keep on being once outside of its universe—would pursue him for the rest of his life.

Finally, wept out, needing to talk to one of his own friends, he called John and Merle in Wisconsin. He hadn't spoken to them since they had returned from Brazil—they had gone on to John's university lecture tour in Chile and had just come home. He knew it would be a shock to them, and he tried to put as much strength and calm as he could into his voice as he rattled off the facts, "Sally died...some mysterious illness... three times in the hospital in a week and a half and she just dies... Nobody knows what the hell even happened..."

"George. Get a hold on yourself. George..." He stopped talking. He took a deep breath. He heard John calling Merle to the telephone with a sense of urgency. "My God, but we should have called you from South America," John said. "Merle...?"

He heard Merle picking up the extension. "George? I'm so sorry. We didn't think." There was a tight, shrill panic in her voice. "We were just about to telephone just in case Sally...George? Are you there? Sally and I went out collecting seashells. You remember? They're the most beautiful shells. Did she bring them home? Because I did and then we discovered there were...things...in them...."

"Things?" he said. "What things?"

"A live hermit crab crawled out of one," John piped in. "There he was just walking across the hotel room floor with a shell on his back..."

"Shush, John! No. Other things. A big brown spidery thing was in one of them. And then we threw the shells into boiling water and all kinds of ugly things came bubbling out..."

He had already set the receiver on its side. Their voices were coming as distantly to him as bird calls, an electronic squawking from across the apartment. Slowly, his heart kicking, he took a long step through the doorway into their bedroom. He saw the tangle of sheets and blankets left from the chaos of the ambulance crew. Then he shifted his attention over, looking at the arrangement of colorful seashells on the night table by Sally's side of the bed. She had set them up in a half circle, spread out like a fan according to colors and size, an exotic rainbow in their design. At the center of the half circle was the large white shell, translucent, shining with its own inner light as though alive.

He didn't know how long he stood in the doorway—ten minutes or two hours—frozen there. Finally, he started toward the bedside. About two strides toward it, suddenly, the white shell moved. Or he saw a flash of something in its mouth, just a tiny jump, enough that he felt a sharp breath fill his lungs with a gasp. He spotted one of his shoes on the floor. Slowly, warily, he bent over to pick it up. He sensed he was being watched. In one quick movement, he hurled the shoe at the night table. The shells were swept clattering over the edge and landed on the floor.

He saw it clearly then—a fast black thing that jumped out of the big white shell. It scuttled quickly backwards across the carpet into the dark under the bed.

He found the shoe again. He got down on his hands and knees. He pulled back the bed ruffle as carefully as he could. He saw it at once, up close, backing away, following the line of the carpet and the wall. He froze, his shoe raised. On impulse, he put the shoe between his teeth. In one violent heave, he lifted the mattress and box spring up and threw them aside. He grabbed the shoe and started chasing the terrible thing. The thing saw him and it knew, black eyes feeling at the air and light, raising up its pincers, its sectioned tail curving upward and toward him, menacing with its sting.

He hammered the shoe wildly against the floor, shouting out in primitive cries of madness and terror. Then it was over. His shoe came down on it several times. The thing was turned into a blue-black smear against the white baseboard. He tossed the shoe away. He collapsed there in the wreckage of the bed frame, crying out why, why, why and lost to the world.

Many years would pass when, at the oddest times, he could feel his dead wife's presence—something he would become aware of suddenly, looking up startled from his work in the lab or while driving in that half-state of fatigue and dreaminess in his car on the crowded four-lane out of Denver. Sometimes, he awoke in the nights with a certainty more vivid than dreams that he had been holding her in their bed, where he slept alone. Often, it was just her voice talking to him, telling him as she so often used to do to pay attention to what was in front of him, to look, watch, see, be aware. George, she would say, *hel*-lo? Where *are* you now? George?

He would always shake off such strange and disturbing sensations as illogical yet common human responses to death—no matter how vivid, it was all in his mind, an irrational compensation.

As for his question why, he was a scientist, after all. All he could finally rely on were explanations from medicine and natural science, as deeply lacking, in symmetry and beauty, as they finally were. The blue scorpion of Brazil—*Scorpionida Tityus Caeruleus*—is a creature of the tropical forests, rarely seen by man and even more rarely ever bothering him. But blue scorpions often crawl into and hide in dark empty places, crevices in rocks, hollows in logs, even into seashells cast up among the shoreline trees. Usually, the sting of a blue scorpion, one of the more poisonous scorpions known, produces a severe reaction to neurotoxins from which most healthy human beings suffer temporary and localized paralysis but recover in a few days. Multiple or repeated stings can, however—and for highly reactive persons—lead to anaphylactic shock, severe paralysis, even death. Tourists should be warned that seashells collected on beaches in South

America or the Caribbean need to be boiled for at least half an hour before being brought home as souvenirs. Of some places in Brazil, it is said that every other seashell found on the beach contains some living thing.

In his worst moments, he kept repeating in his mind these explanations. And, over the years, like the most distant galactic noise, her voice gradually disintegrated into something close to silence.

The Perfect Wife

(after de Maupassant)

T he limousine ride back to Washington through the green hills of Virginia would have been beautiful but for the indecisive rain. Gray mists were rolling in like smoke from distant fires, languishing over the highway and in the trees. Señor Ramírez stared out a window at this dismal grayness. He held a package from his wife in his lap, wrapped in plain brown paper tied with green string.

He tried to make sense of the landscape, so different, so distant from the red craggy mountains and desert of his native Catamarca in Argentina. As the driver slowed with caution on what felt to him were spongy brakes on the slick pavement, Señor Ramírez concluded that the dark mood of the weather reflected his own. "Good. Let it rain then," he thought bitterly.

He remembered the snickering comment of Contreras, a special attaché from the Argentine embassy, an undersecretary of his country in charge of multilateral business deals, a tone in his voice like a teenager on his way to a bordello. "Well, well, Sergio... Who back in Catamarca could imagine that pretty little sophisticated woman, so soft, so glamorous, the redhead who speaks such wonderful Spanish and who always seemed so friendly to us all, was not really the economist's wife?"

The economist's wife. She had been a source of energy and help to the economist, without a doubt, constantly at his side even as they toured the most remote little towns in the dry foothills of the Andes. Just one easy glance from her dark green eyes, one toss of her naturally red hair, could easily capture the men. But her real duty had been with their wives, hour after hour spent with wives of members of the provincial Chambers of Commerce, wives' auxiliaries of so many Rotary Club chapters, even with the factory women from the sneaker plant at Sunday company barbecues. Yes, she had done real duty at those endless lunches and barbecues and parties, had tasted and praised the local wine, had even read stories and helped with puppet shows for the children, four weeks on tour with the economist, persuading and selling "the project" to the women as if she and her husband always knew that it would be the wives who would eventually hold the most sway in final decisions.

What had been required was truly monumental, convincing hundreds of people in his remote desert state and the neighboring states of Jujúy and Salta to give away so much land and so many resources for what amounted to a mere few cents in promised fees to what had become known only as "the project" almost everywhere. This project was an international gas pipeline that would run all the way from the south of Argentina up through the spine of South America, a massive gas highway to be built across plains and deserts, over the Andes mountains, pushing its way through jungles and spanning numerous difficult streams and rivers into Bolivia, Peru and Brazil. Señor Ramírez had devoted a good part of nine years of his life to this, sincerely convinced it was for the ultimate benefit and progress of his state, his country, his continent, his people, faithful of the prelature of *Opus Dei*, "with the greatest possible competence, for the glory of God and the service of others, contributing to the sanctification of the world."

Sergio Ramírez knew his own self-interest was at stake, too, that he stood to make a small fortune—and why not for so many years of dedicated work—since he would be extremely influential in the awarding and management of contracts for the construction and would have a permanent interest in operating his leg of the pipeline when it was finished. Still, the financing for the whole deal ultimately depended on the United States. And the United States counted on the direct participation of a single influential economist, Dr. Jon Giordano. Before giving his approval, this Dr. Giordano in turn had to be assured of the contracts to give land and resources away almost for free. So began a kind of political campaign to which Señor Ramírez had devoted so many years, and the results for which this Dr. Giordano and his beautiful wife from the United States had finally held the keys.

His wife. The beautiful Jane. She won them all over with her charm and ability to reach out to them in their language. She was filled with suitable words for all, even drawing out sewing patterns of the latest fashions in New York at rustic, woven-straw tables with the poorest of the farming women. And she seemed to be always so in love with Dr. Giordano, international banking vice-president of Americorp, ex-member of the President's Council of Economic Advisors of the United States, more than an influential voice in all decisions of the International Monetary Fund regarding South America. This Jane had clung to his arm during the many public events as they toured the deserts and jungles. She seemed always at his hair or brushing the dust off his three-piece suit. She gazed proudly at him as he gave his endless series of dull speeches in a somnambulant monotone outlining statistical projections of progress in "the overall transition from state-owned industries to privatization in the new democracies," then recited his calculations asserting how the project would create thousands of jobs in the "new international marketplace of globalization."

Those looks Jane gave him were so full of happiness and love that it was almost impossible not to share her feelings toward her husband. And her own charming effect on the endless ceremonies of such a massive business deal surely went a long way toward convincing even the most conservative townspeople and villagers and petty officials, finally, to a man—it was almost too incredible to believe there had not in the end been a single hold-out in such an intricate scheme—to sacrifice a swath of land, at least an acre on each side and in some places more, virtually for pennies, almost nothing in rents payable only in a remote and barely conceivable future for this pipeline that would run like a long black sutured scar up the back of almost half the continent. And it was astonishing how this Jane had had such an effect—how she had been worshipped like a movie star wherever she went, how her brilliant, affable personality had somehow influenced more than anything else that the backers of the project would finally win.

But this wasn't the half of what bothered Sergio Ramírez, rancher and businessman from what he knew was just a backwater of the world, nevertheless a savvy politician. He had always considered himself as tough and wary as a pampas fox in his business dealings. He expected lies, deceptions, disillusionments, though always it had been a matter of his personal morality never to practice such manipulations on others.

No, what bothered him about it was that his own wife, Isabel, had been so taken with this woman introduced to them as Jane. The two had quickly become inseparable companions, in no time, it seemed, leaning against each other's shoulders, arms around each other's waists, trading intimate whispers at social events, then laughing in that way women did when they shared secrets men would never know. They had gone horseback riding together on long weekends while he and Dr. Giordano had pored over maps, charts and spread-sheets in the office. It was Isabel who had shown Jane proudly around the green ranch and fields he and his father and grandfather had carved out of the desert with their own hands, then the processing plant and oil and gas trucking company that Señor Ramírez had managed to build with his dedicated labor and influence out of almost nothing. Then again, Jane had continually sung his own praises to Dr. Giordano, a man at best strangely noncommittal and slightly off-putting for his formality in almost everything. At the same time, this Jane was capable of the most feminine domesticity. She and Isabel took long excursions with the children up into the mountains. They went to mass together on Sundays, where Isabel reported she was able to give the responses to prayers in perfect Spanish. She spent mornings with Isabel supervising the cooks and trading recipes, a full partner in the many banquets they were hosting as a big part of their campaign. Looking back on it now, he thought Isabel and this Jane had spent far, far too much time together, unnaturally long hours off in the fields. The two women had become intimate friends, or so it had seemed, no doubt complaining to each other about their workaholic husbands, the price they paid for such successful men with their dreams. They ended their five weeks spent almost continually together calling each other sister, promising to write and telephone. "What a woman!" Isabel said. "Such charm! Such real class! Do you see how she speaks Spanish with hardly a yanqui accent? And independent? We could learn so much in this country from a woman like her!"

The limousine slowed again, boating through the foggy rain of northern Virginia, Señor Ramírez glancing up at the rearview mirror to find the black liveried driver also looking at him. Señor Ramírez frowned and shook his head. He had no idea what he meant to signal to the driver by that shaking of his head, but the driver quickly shifted his eyes back at the road as if in apology for intruding. Señor Ramírez wasn't a man used to riding in limousines, always preferring his own car, or buses or taxis, but as one of the managers of the project, he had decided that day he had better look his part.

What foolishness, he thought. What a ridiculous waste. He was mindful again of how tightly he still gripped the parcel in his lap. He thought of how lovingly it had been put together for this Jane by his wife. He understood there was a jar of homemade *dulce de leche* Isabel had cooked herself, a kind of caramel candy sauce Jane had fallen in love with; packages of *mate* tea likewise; and, knitted by his wife's own hands out of wool from Sergio's own flocks of sheep, matching pairs of woolen slippers with complicated *indio* designs which this Jane had seen on the feet of the servants and remarked on for their quaintness and simple beauty. His wife had knitted this woman slippers! It was hard to believe. And she had no doubt written a long, friendly letter included in the package. For a moment, he resisted a curious impulse to tear the package open and read his wife's letter. But he would never violate her privacy. A sound marriage was above all based on trust. And what good would reading it do now?

Suddenly, he was angry beyond control. He slammed the parcel against his thigh, hard. One corner of the brown paper split under the string. He just couldn't get over the memory of Isabel so joyfully asking him to bring this little gift to Jane. "Make sure it gets to her," Isabel said. "If you don't see her yourself, insist that the economist deliver it. Promise? Sergio? Are you listening?"

He had said he would. Well, it wouldn't be the first time he had disappointed her. Señor Ramírez was struck with the full outrage of what had been put over on him, on his friends, his family, on almost every citizen of Catamarca. The violation he felt at the very idea of it made him taste the bitter, churning bile burning in his stomach most of the afternoon. He felt as if he had spent five weeks entertaining thieves.

The thought that this economist Giordano's "wife" had been a hired actress made him want to tell the driver to turn the car around so he could go back to challenge the man to a fist fight. And the actress? For her, it must have been like a delightful holiday, four weeks with all expenses paid in South America and the chance to be at the center of the attention and applause of thousands of people. What more did an actress need? And she had played her part so brilliantly, the savvy and charming wife of the dull economist, the ultra-scientific banker with his hieroglyphic computer programs and complicated math, the woman who knew better than he the ways of the world and the quickest and most direct means into a whole country's pockets. She must have enjoyed herself. Sure. Everything she did had an air of adventure and joy attached to it that actually infected all who came near her almost perfect and exuberant beauty.

Señor Ramírez could see it all—the dryland peasant farmers who had hardly known how to do more than sketch out an

"X" as their signatures lining up with hats in hand in front of the banquet table where they nodded and grinned in response to the benevolent smiles from this Jane as if she were a kind of queen. Even more pathetic were the elaborate and mincing bourgeois flourishes of the village mayors who strutted around in front of her like gamecocks with their souvenir pens. And even worse were the pretentious airs of the self-important petty national officials who administered the vast wilderness of state-owned lands, all of them signing up, too, after a spirited dance, one dance with her was all it took for them. He remembered them all as so impressed by her that one giving smile and graceful kiss on the cheek might have been enough for them to sign away their lives.

And what of the economist? What really was her role with him? Señor Ramírez knew from the reports of his maids that when Jon Giordano and his glamorous "wife" stayed at the ranch they had all but laid aside their pretense. They were more like feverish kids together than husband and wife. They coaxed and cooed at each other like passionate lovers, slept in the same bed, always roughed up the sheets. Sounds of their love-making rang out through the big ranch house during one afternoon siesta. Isabel remarked on the noise they made during Sergio's uneasy rest after another heavy meal. She said, "See? And they've been together how long?"

The way she punched the words *cuánto tiempo*, how long, had a sarcastic bite which he tossed off as one of her usual barbs when she pointed out other happy-seeming couples, though she was gentle enough about it, supportive wife that she was—faithful, obedient, devoted to a good Catholic life within the sacrament of marriage. And he believed it was a solid marriage, built on a far more abiding foundation than mere physical passion. Theirs had been an old-fashioned union of the kind rarely seen, even in their day, arranged by their parents, really, though as children, Sergio and Isabel had grown up like close cousins. He remembered how they had run barefoot together, how they had captured toads in the red dirt at Sunday barbecues, piling them on each other's backs in little corrals made of sticks; he recalled vividly how their parents had tossed them into the same outdoor bathtub to scrub them off before taking either one of them home, naked babies splashing together with innocent glee. Later, they were paired up at country folk dances more like a brother and sister act than a couple. They were encouraged to date in groups of teens, according to tradition, under the watch of an older sister acting as chaperone—only petting and cautious fondling allowed, which of course made them eager for more. Ever since they could remember, they were told they were meant for each other—the De Vigo family with all sisters, the Ramírez family with two sons, and Sergio was the eldest, his younger brother, as was the custom then, sent off to a military academy and the officer corps, the Air Force, in his case, to avoid as much as possible the taint of the dictatorship, the branch of the military perhaps least involved. Also, Juan Carlos had always enjoyed driving too fast on back country roads, becoming a pilot was one of his childhood ambitions. Juan Carlos then martyred himself to the delirious folly of that same dictatorship, one of the first pilots shot down in his Mirage IIIF fighter-bomber during the catastrophic war with the British for the Islas Malvinas, in 1982, little more than ten years before, a loss Sergio often thought had cast a pall over the early years of his marriage. What a humiliating folly for such a sacrifice, the dictatorship didn't even have the balls to announce defeat—village women continued to knit sweaters and blankets for the draftees for weeks afterwards in a show of patriotism which Señor Ramírez had encouraged and admired, as he had supported also the first years of harsh national discipline the ruling junta had imposed. He assured himself that, according to his faith, such sacrifices were actions that maintained the order of the universe, but, deep down, he had to admit he felt differently—Juan Carlos, his only brother, fast-driving Juan Carlos—then news surfaced proving other crimes of the dictatorship, the kidnappings, the tortures, the tens of thousands of murdered and "disappeared," for which he also started blaming himself, a feeling like his heart had been ground down into a choking red dust, throbbing puffs of some excruciating granular haze inside his chest that made it painful for him to breathe. As if financial gain could compensate for such personal loss, Sergio then redoubled his devotions to building the fortunes of their families—his and Isabel's—and in his brother's memory.

Before this had happened, by his marriage to Isabel, nearby lands were united into one, as it used to be during the centuries of *latifundios*, though neither family could claim such social position nor that much land no matter how much they pretended to such fantasies—both were third-generation immigrants, with grandparents off the boat from Galicia who had earned stakes working a *la golondrina*, as it was called, like swallows, flitting from harvest to harvest in the pampas until they saved up enough to buy spreads in the northern desert. And so two medium-sized, dryland ranches were stitched together into one larger holding both more manageable and survivable as a result of this wedding of the grandchildren. "A classic example of a friendly merger to create an economy of scale," Dr. Giordano had commented at dinner one night after Isabel told the story of how they married. Sergio swallowed his laughter when he realized the man didn't mean it as a joke.

During the ceremony at the cathedral, and at the reception—in all that posing with each other and their families for the photographer—Isabel played her part, austere and subdued, a virgin all wrapped up in her nervous expectations, shyly glancing at her white pearlized shoes. But later, in their suite at the Hotel Mundo, it was Isabel who stripped her veil and let loose with a lewd little laugh, who sent down to room service for cognac instead of the traditional champagne. The same way as kids they once wrestled in the grass, she reached for him eagerly, as assured and confident as any bar girl pro his father had set Sergio up with in his youth—that traditional initiation rite for country boys while on trips showing livestock at La Rural in Buenos Aires. This was not the innocent bride he had expected. He asked no questions. He wasn't disappointed. It all felt natural, like the logical extension of their childhood play. And so it had been ever since—Isabel in the lead, all at her urgings in the bedroom, with her indulgences in mail-order lingerie from the United States, long frilly things "to hide my hips," as she said. She thought she was too broad in the hips. He liked her ample hips, preferred they not be hidden, but he said nothing—as long as she was happy. Everywhere else, he ran the show as was fitting to his station. He thought himself a contented man. Born to them so far were a daughter and a son, and they weren't finished yet, so who could complain?

"Hear that? The guest bed sounds like a trampoline," Isabel said.

"I'll send a man in later to tighten up the frame."

Under the covers, he felt his wife's hand reach playfully around into his boxer shorts. From the wall over the carved oak bureau across the room—his chest of drawers—a portrait of Father Josemaría Escriva, "the Saint of the Ordinary," as

Pope John Paul II had beatified him, stared out at their bed, the priest's face framed by an exaggerated yellow halo of sunlight, his searching gaze through heavily framed glasses like a call to duty. Sergio sleepily moved Isabel's hand away—he was tired, he needed rest, mindful of social chores he had to be sharp for later, when they would host members of the Agrarian Association. The brutal summer heat of Catamarca blew over him through the humming window fans, lazy heat that made him want to sink into the damp sheets like a horse lies down in the stockpond mud. He turned to his wife and, with a tired sigh, he squeezed her hand. He pressed his body close against her back. He kissed her neck, her hair, her cheek, assuring her of his affections. He said, "Please, my love, not now. It's hard even to think with this pressure. Let's just rest. I promise, when all the complexity of this biggest business deal in the history of this whole country is finally completed..."

"Be careful, Sergio. One day, we'll look in the mirror and discover we've grown old all at once," she said.

More than just stirring up Isabel, this Jane had captured the hearts of all of Catamarca and beyond. The afternoon the last easement was granted, the last land contract signed and delivered, there was a huge festival and party in the capital that kept going until early the next morning. As Jane was invited by the governor to mount the platform with Dr. Giordano in the old Spanish square decorated with crepe paper flags of all five countries involved in the project, a crowd greeted her with joyous shouts like they would a movie idol or a rock star. There were fireworks. The governor moved over to a big red switch and invited Jane to share the honor of setting off the first rocket. Afterward, there was dancing in the moonlit plaza, and she could be seen in an elegant yet revealing evening gown still dazzling the local officials who had worked for the project, her gift to each a final dance. And when it came time for them to leave, to climb into their hired car which would take them to the airport and a private jet to fly them home, three little girls dressed in white and looking as if they were ready to be confirmed walked out onto the platform. The little girls in white recited pretty patriotic poems they had written, it seemed, both for her and for their country. Jane kissed the girls. She grabbed Dr. Giordano's hand and raised it up in hers like the winner of a prizefight. As the black Mercedes carried the economist and his beautiful wife slowly away from the plaza, the women waved their fans and handkerchiefs and the men their hats, everyone shouting and cheering happy goodbyes. Jane rolled down her car window and waved back to them with tears in her eyes. She blew kisses to the crowd and shouted, "*¡Adiós! ¡Hasta luego!* Goodbye! See you all soon!"

Of course, the economist had invited Señor Ramírez and other important functionaries in the business deal to visit his home in Virginia if they came to the United States. Though he had not said so at the time, Señor Ramírez did have infrequent reasons to go to Washington—most of them involving his work with Rotary Clubs International or with small-scale trade possibilities on behalf of Catamarca that he pushed with embassy officials he knew, and recently, he had become a member of and valued contributor to the Andes Foundation, which had an office in Washington. It was inevitable that a day would come when he would accept the invitation.

He had called on his third day in town and was invited to this party. Nothing in his life compared to the strange shock he felt after arriving at the Virginia mansion, Isabel's brown parcel in his hands. The occasion was an afternoon luncheon and what was supposed to have been a pleasant Spring garden party for selected members of the international business and banking community. The whole thing had been moved indoors because of the rain. Señor Ramírez wandered through the large rooms of the colonial house among a crowd of as many as eighty or ninety guests. Most of them were Latin American business and political leaders and a few of their wives who had occasion to be in Washington, here and there a few generals and colonels he recognized out of uniform. Of course, more than anyone else, Señor Ramírez kept searching for the economist's wife.

"Why, there she is," the Argentine undersecretary named Contreras had finally said, pointing toward the end of a long buffet table where a handsome, older woman with ash blonde hair seemed busily discussing a detail of the food service with one of the waiters. "That one there is Mrs. Giordano," he said, barely fighting back a quick grin as at a practical joke. "Jane Giordano."

Señor Ramírez almost let the parcel drop from his hands. When he was assured a second then even a third time that this elegant yet otherwise unremarkable woman was, indeed, Jane Giordano, he felt a ringing in his ears and a strange off-balance sensation that made him afraid he might actually fall down. He felt a sudden desperate urge to say something but couldn't find the words. "Oh, yes, well," Contreras said in a conspiratorial tone. "This one is rather different from the other one. She doesn't speak one word of Spanish. But you still see she's quite at home."

"But…it can't be," was all Señor Ramírez said.

It was then that Contreras made his comment about the other "wife" in that locker-room tone of voice, as though letting him in on some off-color joke. All the while, Señor Ramírez was observing this other Mrs. Giordano, a stiff-looking woman, the kind of woman who shook hands only fully at arm's length and who seemed to stick her nose in the air at everyone. She assumed a posture at this party of only appearing to fuss over the comfort of her Hispanic guests while looking them over like a coarse gang of escaped convicts who had turned up mistakenly in her home.

Suddenly, Dr. Giordano appeared at her side—good old conservative Jon, still in a dull blue jacket even at a party in his own house. Señor Ramírez watched him greet this other wife with a courteous and dispassionate nod. The two of them began to circulate formally around the big banquet room, then out into the colonial living room with drinks in their hands.

"I… Please, Contreras," Señor Ramírez finally said. "This is taking me a moment to absorb. You mean to say that this man, this Dr. Giordano, actually thinks he can get away with this? What does he imagine? That because we live in such a remote and provincial place that we would never get to Washington and actually see him and…his wife? He must be crazy…"

By this time, Minister Contreras was leading him to a small couch and sitting him down. The undersecretary waved at a waiter for drinks. Then with a kind of easy shrug and a tone of voice like he was initiating Sergio into the rules of a private club, he explained everything.

"A lot of people know," Contreras said. "Or at least almost everyone at this party. Imagine. An esteemed man like Dr. Giordano, a great economist, expert in international finance, a highly paid consultant for all of our countries, not to mention his own. How much of the year do you think he spends traveling? One-third, one-half of the time, I would guess. And to have a wife like this one, this other Jane, who actually hates to travel, and who wouldn't dream of spending a night in a hotel that didn't have at least five stars…You understand what I'm saying? So what does he do? He finds himself another wife—just for that purpose, just for what she does—the redhead, the one you and everybody else really love, the other one, also named Jane. And this other Jane really was quite a good stage actress in her time, in New York, Los Angeles, here in Washington. So from her point of view, you might say she landed herself a more permanent role—you get my meaning? Dr. Giordano must pay her a fortune, you understand, even quite possibly a percentage of his own enormous fees. Not to mention the fact that, as far as anyone can tell, she travels with him as completely devoted to him as would the most perfect wife…."

"And…this wife?" Señor Ramírez asked. "This Jane? How could she ever put up with such a thing?!"

"Well, now, that's a different story," said the undersecretary. "As far as I know, nobody ever mentions the other wife to her. I mean, why ruin a good thing? You must admit the other Jane is incredibly valuable not only for him but for everyone involved. Your state of Catamarca isn't the only place in Latin America ready to erect statues of her in the plazas. And the Jane who lives here is such a stuck-up bore that nobody I know gives a damn if she's being deceived. I mean, people have made mistakes, have asked about the wrong Jane in front of this Jane, and this Jane just looks at them like they're incredibly stupid and hides behind her husband. But it's the other one, the Jane you know, everyone wants to see. So, somehow, everyone just keeps quiet until Dr. Giordano takes another trip and brings her along. Then when Jon and the other Jane are visiting our countries, well, what would be the point? How would we ever explain? What would people say?"

What would Isabel say? After a long and perplexed silence, Contreras gave his arm a conspiratorial squeeze. "Don't think too much about this, Ramírez, my friend, my brother. As long as we get our bank loans, who cares who the man is sleeping with?"

Señor Ramírez wanted to spit in the economist's face, or slap him loudly in front of everyone, demand of him some answer to how he could go around deceiving so many innocent people, most of all Isabel. He feared there would come a moment when he was all but forced to exchange greetings with the economist, though he avoided it, even getting up and moving into a different room until he could calm his rage. After all, there were far more than mere personal relations at stake. When the moment did come, running into the two by accident in the large hall while he was on his way to leaving without a word, all Señor Ramírez finally managed to do was shake hands coldly with the economist and say, intending his words to be barbed with irony, "So pleased to meet your...your *wife.*"

In Spanish, he might easily have managed his double-meaning. But his tone in English sounded flat and lacking. Dr. Giordano responded as awkwardly stiff and strangely formal as though nothing had happened, nothing had changed. He muttered a few noncommittal words of introduction to his wife, who seemed taller than he was. When the state of Catamarca was mentioned, this Jane intoned a few quaint dismissive words through her nasal passages based on a summary knowledge of a topographical globe, as if location meant everything. "Of course. South America. In the mountains. Rain much there?"

Señor Ramírez was relieved when they moved on to other guests. He discovered he had actually been holding his breath through a forced smile. His heavy parcel under one arm, he quickly made a few excuses to familiar faces he knew from the Argentine embassy and left the party.

On the slow ride through Virginia in the ugly rain, Señor Ramírez stewed and fretted over the two wives of the economist. He suffered a whole range of emotions from violation and outrage to the deepest sadness when he fought off an almost uncontrollable urge to cry. Then suddenly, on impulse, he pressed the button for the back window of the limousine. The window slid open with a hissing sound and he felt an icy, stinging rain in his face. He tossed the parcel he had been carrying all day out into the rain. He stuck his head out and tried to see where the package landed but lost sight of it in the gray mist. He closed the window. Immediately, he regretted what he had just done. He should at least have retrieved Isabel's letter, seen that her gifts went to someone who might appreciate them. He glanced up toward the road. He saw the black driver looking back at him with disapproval in the rearview mirror but the man said nothing.

Señor Ramírez shook his head. He reached for a paper towel in the back of the limousine, dried his face and hands. Somewhere along the way, he realized that he, too, like the rest in his community, would keep his silence. He would make enough money that he and his family could be rich for generations. All he had to give in exchange was finally to join in the network of lies and deceptions running the modern world. More, he would tell his own wife nothing. He would make up some story or excuse—he had left her package on the plane, or on the seat of the limousine, how stupid, could she forgive him? And Jane was out of town, off visiting her family. On the other hand, how close had the two women really become? He wondered. After he told his wife such a story, how could he ever be sure which one of them had been fooled? He thought about this, staring off into the gray mists, early evening sinking into gloom. But no, that was impossible. That much, he was sure his wife would have told him. He would make up some story then. That was the kind thing to do. Let Isabel have her memories of friendship. Let her keep her happy illusions.

Cuban Nights

L et us consider a life—the life of a sculptor and friend, Max Spicer, who so recently died. Let us recall the many winter nights when we gathered at his hospitable table, retiring from the generous meals he presided over to smoke cigars and drink hot rums in his living room. Remember how we listened to Spicer telling and retelling his story as though none of us had ever heard it before, recounting so often the same events with his obsessive energy—the energy of his art, some might say—so we knew just when to laugh or to mourn with him or to keep our silence. Almost all of us gathered here tonight took Max Spicer's words, his outrage, his fascination, so into ourselves that his story became our own. So it falls to us now, missing him as we do this winter night, to tell his story once more—an account of his art and life as well as his strange and fateful experience with Cuba—then to raise our glasses to him one last time in loving memory.

Let us remember the beginning of Max Spicer's career, how, after his studies at the prestigious Art Institute of Chicago, he achieved such a growing reputation in the trendy gallery world of New York. The *Times* and *Art News* referred to him alongside Oldenberg and Rosenquist and even the young

Warhol as part of that early '60s movement which combined conceptual art, pop culture and humorous articles of daily use—brand name labels, cartoon images, photos of movie stars, salvaged floor tiles, washing machine parts, automobile hood ornaments used like religious icons. We can look at photographs from that era—improbable Max Spicer sculptures built to oversized and zany scales, almost all untitled, or only so by the artist's name and a number as was a vogue in those days. Looking at these photos, it's easy to conceive how radical they were at the time.

Spicer's sculptures were early contributions to the postmodern revolution. His constructions often had vacuum cleaner hoses attached to them and connecting them either to parts of themselves or to other constructions. Everything was somehow plugged into everything else in a bizarre parody of practical functioning. And Spicer was one of the first American sculptors to work in form-molded plastics—animal shapes, plastic faces, other body parts that looked almost human jutted out at odd angles from his kinetic contraptions which hummed along crazily powered by the electric motors he installed in them. Cartoonish moons, planets and stars in a kind of combination Alexander-Calder-Rube-Goldberg-like machinery whirled over the viewer's head in what Spicer once described in an interview as mobiles of lunacy and madness.

In his day, Spicer was the artist for some very important installations. There's a three-story clock tower machine that isn't really a clock but moves like one and at last report is still moving in downtown Minneapolis. A steel and ceramic statue with dozens of plastic faces and pseudo-religious symbols—saint's insignias and Protestant crosses with vacuum hoses interconnecting them—guards the entrance to a park in St.

Louis. A spinning planetary whirligig the size of a bulldozer hangs high over the lobby of a corporate bank headquarters in Boston. These are only a few of the impressive monuments for which Max Spicer might be remembered.

We should say here that, no matter what one thought of it as art, a Spicer sculpture was always funny in some way. It made most people laugh or smile, once they saw through their initial response of shocked offense. And his personal image generally had this same effect. His idea of a swank gallery opening where stock brokers and wealthy collectors would be looking over his work was to dress up in costume and make a sculpture of himself. There he was, intimidating and funny at the same time, dressed in a moon suit next to the three-piece suited banker who was buying, Spicer's face framed in a half-moon headdress, his hands holding out menacing-looking scepters with dangling moons. Once, he dressed like a cartoon bandit—in a leotard and leggings with prison stripes, a raccoon mask over his eyes. He attended his posh Madison Avenue show strapped into a working replica of an electric chair upholstered in rattlesnake skin, daring his critics to pull the switch on the wall that might have ended his career, which not one of them ventured to do no matter how much he taunted, of course reinforcing Spicer's contempt for critics he held to all his life.

Max Spicer was both a funny and a somewhat dangerous man, in his own way. And the art world eventually began treating him as a threat in response to these eccentric stunts at his shows long before such so-called *happenings* were in fashion. Or his critics took Spicer less and less seriously the more he made a joke of all of them, of the tap dancing, as he used to call it, when the young artist had to use his personality at gallery shows to help make his reputation in a social milieu mainly filled, according to Spicer, with little more than rich snobs and bores who were slaves to cultural fads and who unfortunately controlled almost everything about an artist's life, work and income if he let them.

Spicer was not about ready to let them. He was really a mild and gentle man until the Philistines, as he called them, made comments on his work. Or worse, if gallery owners or corporate clients didn't present or install his creations in just the right way, he could let loose on them with hideous profanities and—recall how he could get with us at times if he were provoked enough—yes, physical threats, with blowtorches and wrenches, until they called in security guards. Because of this, nervous gallery owners started passing by his work for shows. Spicer knew he was playing out his brief ride of fame and spectacular income from corporate installations when a rubberized construction—the one that looks something like three tons of motorized mating sea turtles, that photo being passed around in front now, yes, that one—was purchased by the architect of a shipping company building in Seattle. The company demanded a provision in the contract that Spicer could only direct the installation long distance. He was not to show up in person. When Spicer saw the photo of the way his work was displayed then complained with loud profanity on the phone, the architect served him with a court order restraining him from ever getting closer than fifty feet to his sculpture or to any employee of the firm. Just at this messy juncture in his career, Spicer had the chance to leave his leased house and studio in Reinbeck on the Hudson he was having increasing difficulty affording. He was invited to spend three years as a distinguished artist in residence hosted by the government of Sweden.

Another point about Max Spicer should be made here. Despite his avant-garde following in that early era of what later became so-called *happenings* and *pop art* and *Gestalt participation* with both the works and artist personalities written up in obscene magazine features as fashionable pioneers of hallucinations from hashish and LSD—what later became what we might call the whole Warholian myth— Spicer was not in any way a part of that scene. He never used drugs. He drank moderately if at all and his only bad habit was cigars. He married the exceptional woman we all know and love—whom he loved and remained faithful to from their wedding night—Tamara, the consummate hostess of our circle, this former fashion model and devoted mother, a woman who, as she tells it, grew bored with the runways and magazine spreads in favor of reading books, raising her four children and taking care of Spicer, more or less in that order of priority.

Tamara Spicer hated the gallery and art party scene. She would stitch up the finishing touches to Spicer's moon suit or bandit costume, drop him off at the train bound for the city and have a hot meal and a warm bed waiting for him when he got home. Spicer often shamelessly pulled out snapshots of his family at shows or client parties and forced them on strangers much in the same way he later did to us and even to his students—disarming people with the incongruity between his often unkempt, unshaven, wild appearance, his coarse language, his very large physical size in person compared to photos of such a normal looking family gathered around a picnic basket, smiling happily at the camera from a neatly mown lawn. Spicer loved his children. He was the one who put them in strollers and papoose packs and herded them off early on Sundays to his nearby Methodist church. And we all know how Tamara was his anchor—in those days, his savior from his obsessions with his work, how he could lose himself for days without sleep or food in the bright sparking showers of blowtorches or bent over the noxious fumes of his plastic form-molding machinery. She rescued him with her set schedule of meals and vitamins, seduced him away from his work into her arms and the happy circle of his family—what a lucky man he always said he was with that beautiful caring wife at his side and his beloved children.

One of the reasons Max Spicer decided to take the invitation for three years in Sweden was Tamara and the kids. Swedish schools were rated among the best in the world. The Swedish government would provide a modern home with a barn-sized studio near the smallish town of Söderhamm on the coast just north of Stockholm, all the raw materials Spicer could dream up to use for his work, a brand new Volvo, some much needed dental care for the kids. And as far as the New York art scene was concerned, it was just the right moment for him to make an honorable escape.

We should recall now how Spicer would, in his diffuse narrative way, tell at this point where his story was going—toward Cuba, unknown to him. Cuba was his direction, his unseen catalyst, his fate, his destiny. How he expressed his astonishment that, even then, Cuba was so mysteriously already working in his life. Cuba was a country and people he had up to then almost no thought of that he could recall. He would ask us to think of it—that Kennedy-era Cuba. Spicer and his family were flying off to Sweden just about the time the CIA with thousands of Cuban expatriates were invading the island's southern coast at the Bay of Pigs, a tragic catastrophe for all concerned. A year and a half later, the brinkmanship of cold war politics concerning

Soviet missiles in Cuba came within twenty minutes of the nuclear destruction of the planet. Cuba became a constant barbed irritation to the government of the United States simply for existing.

As a humiliated President Kennedy publicly declared himself responsible for the blunder at the Bay of Pigs, Spicer and his family were settling into their comfortable home in Söderhamm with its converted barn for a studio that overlooked a fast glistening stream filled with native salmon and lunker brown trout. The villagers welcomed Tamara and the kids into their steady bucolic life. She walked the children each morning to nursery school and kindergarten and back. The shopkeepers were magnanimous toward her crude tries at speaking Swedish as she bought the provisions she experimented with for wild berry cream sauces and deer and elk filets, gray hen fried with spruce twigs, salt codfish and pickled delicacies of all kinds to feed Spicer with—and later on, us, as so many here can so deliciously recall—when she rescued Spicer from his barn.

With his Swedish fellowship, Spicer set to work on a new series of sculptures with a freedom he had never known. He had limitless quantities of high-carbon Swedish steel, tungsten, chrome and other rare or prohibitively expensive but now free materials brought to him by the truckloads. Naturally, his sculptures were growing larger, taller, heavier, even immense—some almost as big as the barn he worked in. And he went wild when he discovered a special Swedish electric motor that was almost noiseless with greaseless bearings guaranteed not to burn out for a quarter century. He mounted, wired and plugged in these high-tech expensive motors everywhere he could to keep the vast absurd machinery of his constructions moving.

The only real job the Swedish government required of Spicer in exchange for all of this was once a week, when Tamara dropped him off at the train station in the brand new Volvo and he rode into Stockholm to look over the work of a gang of art students connected with the Moderna Museet. He advised them on plastic form molding and various casting and welding techniques and often they gave him rides back to Söderhamm. The Spicer house filled with youths in greasy coveralls toasting each other with the cheapest possible vodka and brandy, eating everything in the house, singing happy songs until morning.

Winter was soon on its way. The light of the north country diminished into a near total darkness. One midnight near Christmas, the Spicers turned out with most of the people in Söderhamm to watch a festival of vestal virgins celebrating winter. Young girls dressed up in long white gowns, adorned their hair with spruce crowns and laurels. They carried candles before them in a dancing procession with ancient pagan singing. The townspeople—parents and children and all—followed the beautiful girls dressed in white to the mouth of the stream where it emptied into the fjord. Young men of the village swept fresh pine boughs before them. The Spicers held hands and strolled along through the snow in pleased amazement, pointing out the spectacle to their four children toddling around them and bundled up in their new wool snowsuits. Before them was a scene which Spicer would later describe like a vast living Botticelli of wintry reveling—a mystical dancing whiteness and sparkling light of pagan celebration. Somehow, during this happy procession of the virgins, the Spicer's youngest, a three-year-old named Kevin, slipped out of Tamara's view for a brief few seconds and wandered off into the darkness. Tamara looked down and counted heads. Kevin was missing. With increasing panic, she circled around in the cold night along the bank of the stream and up the hill into the dark woods calling his name.

The ceremony of the virgins soon broke up into the emergency of a village looking for a lost child, some of the girls abandoning their procession to help, their candles raised high under the trees and over the snow. Spicer stayed close to the captain of police, who quickly assembled a crew of well-meaning folk with flashlights and lanterns. Hours went by and dawn came. The boy was discovered almost at the stream's mouth. Swift water and the rocks had torn off his woolen snowsuit. He was drowned, lying naked and face up, caught under an outcropping of stones, his body and hair tangled into a clinging undergrowth of dark green moss.

That mossy chlorine green would make Spicer ill whenever he saw it or even thought about the color for the rest of his life. Tamara and the undertaker spent hours trying to scrub a filmy layer of green off the boy's body and out of his hair before the funeral. Spicer could barely stand by for a few minutes in his black jacket at the service before he vanished from the church. Tamara was the strong one, seeing to all the details of the funeral and cremation—they had decided on cremation so they could one day bring their youngest child's ashes home. She used her skills as a model to perform all the public obligations of grief with grace and elegance for the town, which took the tragedy as fully to heart as if the child had been one of its own. Villagers came in delegation after delegation on courtesy calls to the Spicer home, bringing food and Swedish vodka along with their condolences and prayers.

Spicer couldn't face any of them. He locked himself in his studio, filled floor to ceiling with his sculptures, all of them heavy and huge, scraping the two-story tile roof. He disconnected the electric motors so that all his work stood still. Outside, the Scandinavian winter arrived full force, locking the world in snow and ice and darkness. He sat on the stool at his empty drawing board in that barn for days on end with the lights off, listening to the storms outside, doubled over in fits of inconsolable bitterness and grief. Tamara brought food to him that he wouldn't touch. She begged him to come with her to the house and hold her there so they could grieve together but he kept pushing her away. No matter what she tried, she couldn't get Spicer to come out of his studio. She enlisted the three children they had left—Tom, David and little Jessica—each born a year apart from each other, Tamara's practical idea of bunching them all together when she had decided to conceive them. She sent each child in repeatedly to ask Spicer to come up to the house. She consulted a doctor in town who recommended calling in an ambulance and a medical team. Finally, it was little Jessica who led an exhausted and sleepless Spicer through the snow by his hand into the house and up the stairs to bed.

In the weeks that followed, Spicer recovered enough to sit at the kitchen window looking out into the snow. Or sometimes, he walked along the stream bank to its icy mouth and stared down into the dark green stones until the stream finally choked with ice and the fjord froze over and there was nothing more to see. There was no question about his working. Swedish government officials relieved him of his once-a-week conservatory teaching, sending a compassionate letter and even an extra foundation check to help with the expenses of death. But it was soon clear to Tamara that Spicer's fellowship in Sweden had come to an early end. She explained her desire to get them all back home safely to New York before anything else might happen. Spicer agreed. He informed the Swedish foundation. As a parting sort of gift, the fellowship committee came up with even more money to purchase one of Spicer's sculptures at a price high enough to pay for the family's move and the exporting by ship of his barn-full of heavy constructions he had completed before his child had drowned.

For the first time, Spicer didn't concern himself with the installation. A few students at the conservatory did the best they could, choosing a sculpture and seeing it installed, rewiring its electric motor—the photo here doesn't do it justice. It's a kind of insect-like steel and plastic machine that kicks what might be legs or arms out behind it in a strange disorienting rhythm, and to this day, the sculpture can be seen at work in one of the side rooms of the Moderna Museet. As for the rest, Spicer used up half the wood in the Söderhamm lumberyard to crate up his sculptures, all the while complaining bitterly that he had chosen the most burdensome and ruinous kind of artist to be in his life, as he used to tell his students in his moments of despair. Who else needs to rent eighteen-wheeler trucks and warehouse space costing what amounted to at least an extra yearly salary just to move and store so much junk he called his art?

Still, as he was supervising the carpentry and cranes and trucks for the move, Spicer began to see his work differently. The idea that he had somehow sacrificed his youngest child for this work—the guilt and bitterness of that obsessive thought—settled in his mind. He lost any vision whatsoever of his huge unusual constructions as art. They became for him instead creations which could never have anything more than the most personal kind of value. He resolved that the sculptures that remained could never be displayed, could never be sold. He envisioned hiding them away somewhere only accessible to himself, renting a special building to house them in no matter what that might cost, taking them on as personal burdens, a lifelong debt that could never be repaid. He would visit his sculptures on special days when he felt the need and keep them up with the same reverence that anyone else might attend to a family grave.

The Spicer family gathered to watch four bright red shipping containers the size of railroad cars packed with the sculptures and loaded by crane into the hold of the steamship Kristianstad, which flew the Swedish flag. Then in a last-minute decision which left Tamara no room for argument, instead of flying home, Spicer decided to pay much cheaper passage for two of six inadequate passenger staterooms on the ship and sail them all back to the United States. The family boarded the ship and left Stockholm harbor with the grieving sense they were riding procession with so many huge red coffins out of respect for the dead.

Two days out of Boston harbor, where the Kristianstad was due to unload, the ship's Captain, a man named Axelsson, received shocking news by radio—the United Federation of Longshoremen and Warehousemen of the United States had just declared a national strike for higher wages. All ports on the East Coast were suddenly shut down. Nothing could be unloaded off any ship until the strike was resolved, which promised to take weeks, laying off tens of thousands of workers, paralyzing shipping in the worst economic disaster to hit the U.S. maritime trades since the Great Depression. Captain Axelsson received orders from Stockholm that what cargo he had for the United States would have to be carried in his hold and off-loaded at his next port of call. This decision was made in an atmosphere of considerable panic—ships had cargoes consigned to them months in advance, and there was only one thing worse than steaming around with an empty hold and that was steaming around with a full hold that couldn't be unloaded. In order not to go bankrupt, some shipping companies resorted to deep-sixing whole cargoes out to sea and letting insurance companies take care of the losses. Under those conditions, the fact that the Kristianstad's owners even allowed the ship to continue on without dumping its U.S.-bound cargo in the Atlantic should have been considered a blessing.

Captain Axelsson sent for Spicer and told him the news as pleasantly as possible, reading the strike notice to him word for word. But Spicer turned apoplectic—the way on occasion so many of us later knew him ourselves—losing control as he once had with his so-called Philistines. He let loose strings of profanities in English and Swedish. Captain Axelsson must have feared even for his physical safety with this very large and apparent madman in a rage on his bridge. With stiff formality, two burley pursers at his side, he ordered Spicer and his family immediately off his ship into a pilot boat which would take them to Boston harbor where they could land.

Calmer, trying to reestablish the now lost sense of comradery he and the Captain had shared during the voyage, Spicer asked about the fate of his cargo. He knew the Kristianstad had been bound from Boston to other American ports—Charleston, then on to Jacksonville and New Orleans— but what was the next foreign harbor where the ship was going? Havana harbor, answered Captain Axelsson. Sweden was a neutral country. There were no cold war boycotts in Sweden. The Kristianstad delivered steel, industrial parts and assorted Russian cargoes to Havana. In Cuba, the ship was loaded with rum, sugar and the best cigars in the world bound for Sweden. As for Spicer's cargo, the captain said he would do his best. He would try to sail the sculptures back to Stockholm and store them there. But he promised nothing. With the authority of his two pursers at his side, he hurriedly ushered Spicer and his family down the ladder into the pilot boat. Captain Axelsson set his course for Cuba.

As many of us recall, Max Spicer could imitate a heavy Swedish accent like no one else. At this point on his Cuban nights, he would parody in his deep voice the guttural swallowed vowels and sing-song tone of Captain Axelsson— Spicer's face turning bright red with the pressure of his laughter barely contained. We laughed with him. This was always a high point of the evening. Then Spicer would serve up another round of brown rum and beer, Tamara urging us on to second helpings of the spicy Cuban food she served—*moros y cristianos*, rice and black beans with chopped onions, avocados, *delicato mango salsa* and tomato *sofrito* as condiments. We passed dishes of her famous lime baked chicken with a *habañero* pepper sauce, *flan casera* for dessert. After the meal, we then followed Spicer into his living room, where he brought out his stock of premium *candela* wrapper cigars from his illegal supply. He played tapes of lively *mambo* and *salongo* music. Ah, what nights. What marvelous Cuban nights, all of us settling back into the warmth and high spirits of Spicer's hospitality, so contentedly listening as he would continue telling his story.

Six weeks after that lonely boat ride into Boston harbor, Max Spicer sadly watching his sculptures sailing off to sea behind him, he received a letter from the Swedish shipping firm informing him that the Cuban government had seized all U.S.-bound cargo aboard the Kristianstad when it had put in at Havana. There was little further explanation. Spicer heard speculations that, in the bellicose atmosphere following the

Cuban missile crisis, Castro and his Peoples' Ministry of Trade considered this and many other seizures of cargoes orphaned by the Longshoremen's strike as a kind of retaliation for the way U.S. Customs so often intervened and prevented Cuban-bound cargoes from reaching its shores. The United States was ruthlessly indiscriminate in its embargo and influential with other nations, doing all it could to cut off shipments of replacement parts for machinery, vital raw materials, things like common light bulbs, early on, even medicines, hospital equipment, infant formulas—anything necessary to run the tiny nation. Spicer was informed that his four huge containers of sculptures had been unloaded in Havana and declared property of the revolution.

Spicer spent months making trips to Montreal and back to petition the Cuban consulate there to get his sculptures returned. The Cuban government's eventual version of events was that the Kristianstad had simply dumped his sculptures off onto a dock, abandoning them without authorization. The Cubans were more than willing to give Spicer back his art, provided he could pay a hard currency fee for dockside labor and storage charges. Spicer then spent more months traveling to Washington to do everything he could to get around U.S. Government trade restrictions and arrange for his sculptures to leave Havana and land somewhere in the United States. He even proposed that he could have them transshipped at great expense through some intermediate European or Latin American port. He got nowhere with these efforts. As far as the U.S. State Department and the U.S. Customs and Immigration Agency were concerned, trade embargo rules against any business whatsoever done with Cuba were firm. No matter the special circumstances, what would happen, they asked, if Spicer were allowed to do some kind of intermediate port transaction for a cargo originating in Cuba? Wouldn't everyone else with an interest in Cuban products feel at liberty to do the same? Despite petition after petition and stacks of letters from the most noted art critics in the world, embargo regulations against trade with Cuba just could not be overcome. No cargo of any kind which originated in Cuba would be allowed into the United States.

At this point in his story, as Tamara was straining another round of killer Cuban espresso through a sock-like contraption, Spicer would rummage through cabinets in his living room and lay out folder upon folder bursting with paperwork. The quantity was unbelievable—stacks of folders covered his glass coffee table and grew out across the floor around the sofa. He would tell us of the day he grew so desperate and frustrated that he recklessly threatened the life of a terrified State Department official at the Caribbean desk. He was led off in handcuffs, a lucky man that the charges were finally dropped by the traumatized bureaucrat. So many of us here— having sat through numerous heated and profane committee meetings with Spicer—can well imagine. Spicer would then tell us how he made the decision to give up his citizenship. He planned to arrange the shipment of his sculptures to Mexico, where he intended that he and his family would emigrate and become citizens if his cargo of precious works ever managed to land in that country.

Tamara put a stop to that idea. Things had gotten bad enough, she would explain—she had no desire for another experiment in international living. Besides, they were nearly broke. Spicer had managed to spend almost all the money they had on attorneys and taking trips to Montreal and Washington, unable to work or do anything but fill out forms and petitions and write letters trying to set his sculptures free.

His works had by that time achieved in the art and diplomatic worlds almost the same kind of notoriety combined with institutional neglect as do most political prisoners.

So it was that Spicer embarked on his long voyage to Cuba. We can imagine what it was like then. U-2 spy planes made daily passes over the island. FBI agents under Hoover dogged the heels of just about any suspicious person who spoke Spanish with a Cuban accent. And from jungle watchtowers on the island it was still unclear that any day a new invasion might be launched by the CIA from bases in Central America. In the '60s there weren't even many regular scheduled flights into Cuba save from airports in the Soviet Union or a few old propeller driven planes which took off at erratic times out of Mexico City and Montreal. Still, Spicer finally resolved to risk his life, scrape together his last spare money, say good-bye to Tamara and his kids and try his luck in Cuba. He arranged a quick visa with the consulate in Canada and bribed his way into a seat on an unscheduled flight out of Montreal. He flew off to Cuba with no idea how he would ever get home.

At José Martí airport, Spicer was interrogated as a potential spy. Only after he signed papers declaring he was a political refugee from imperialism was he finally allowed to enter Cuba. The first thing he did was to visit his sculptures. How amazed he was to find them still intact, taken carefully out of the containers and wooden crates by the hand labor of what must have been dozens of *obreros* using thick ropes and huge wooden rollers to move such towering tons of weight—Spicer described this as a labor rivaled only by moving the great stones for the pyramids. So there they all were, his Swedish period constructions, standing two stories high apiece, fifteen in all bunched together on a remote wooden pier which only miraculously held up their weight. They must have looked like a weird forest of steel, tungsten, chrome and plastic conceptual shapes jutting out into the fetid harbor of old Havana. But what in the world was Spicer going to do with them?

On his Cuban nights, down off the wall of his drafty Victorian living room came Spicer's most prized photograph which he delighted in passing from guest to guest—yes, the one in the black frame being passed around now. There he is, Max Spicer with Fidel Castro, *El Jefe* dressed in his characteristic green fatigues and billed campaign cap, gazing with evident admiration at the big *yanqui* artist in his ragged blue jeans, dirty sneakers, grease-stained T-shirt burned through with holes from his welder's sparks. And take note of Spicer, in all respects a revolutionary now, his long hair sticking out wildly from under a cocked Che Guevara beret with its red star. This photo was taken at the ceremony in the courtyard of the modern National Schools of Art at Cubanacán Beach, when Spicer celebrated his gift to Cuba of his sculptures. In the shadows behind them, obviously too big to fit fully into the photo, we can barely see a small piece of a mammoth fishlike construction with its collection of moons, stars, planets for eyes, the nose of a plastic cow's face staring out from its fish's belly. Fidel Castro presented to him on this occasion the certificate of gratitude framed in brushed steel— that one, like a hammer-and-sickle embossed diploma in elaborately lettered old Spanish script—declaring Max Spicer forever a friend of the Cuban people.

The installation at the National Schools of Art took care of only one of Spicer's fifteen sculptures. He then spent months at work with his patched together crew of *mulato* laborers, painfully levering and rollering the other fourteen monstrous heavy things off the rickety pier and into Russian army trucks. He and his work crew then very slowly drove each one to a selected location somewhere on the island, really just to where Spicer could finally get permission from various local party committees. It wasn't easy for a postmodern Spicer construction to find a home in a place so dominated by busy baroque facades, so many fluted columns and arches and elaborately painted tiles or in the narrow streets and open antique courtyards of the Spanish colonial architecture found almost everywhere in Cuba.

How Spicer would laugh—and how we laughed with him—at the folly of it all, at this very photo he passed around of the sculpture which looks something like the skeleton of an old umbrella wired so it would be perpetually jerking open and closed that he set up in a small plaza across from the art nouveau Fausto Theater in old Havana. Or the one that looks like some kind of monstrous grasshopper that he talked the new Communist Party management team of the Tropicana into allowing to lean out from among the sheltering palms of its poolside gardens. There's the large, mostly exposed-girder sculpture that he stood up rather unobtrusively next to the big Ferris wheel in Lenin Park, where it whirled around in counter motion. Others he simply resorted to dumping off along highways in tropical rural settings leading into the towns of Matanzas, Cardenas and Pedro Betancourt—as we can see, somehow like metaphors for communism itself, shapes easily mistaken for industrial or highway equipment always working away in exactly the same place but never really accomplishing anything. He set the smallest piece up on an outcropping of stones near the tail end of the Malacón sea wall, where it kept jerkily spreading its chrome wings like a dying bird. This other, slightly larger construction once sat in the sand on the beach at Miramar, proving generally useful to bathers there looking to get shade from the sun. His last and biggest sculpture took two Russian army trucks and eventually three teams of oxen when one of the trucks broke down to haul across the mountains through what turned out to be a near hurricane-strength storm so that Spicer could set it up—yes, that one that looks something like the spinning tower of an apocalyptic clock—in what he discovered later was an abandoned zoo park on the outskirts of Santiago.

So it was that it took six hard laborious months before Spicer finally installed all fifteen of his sculptures with nearly impossible toil from one end of the island to the other, from Pinar del Rio to Santiago. By that time, he had more than worn out his haphazard crew, not to mention all remaining patience of the Peoples' Militia liaison team which had generously supplied him with so much desperately needed Russian gas and equipment for the monumental moves. The very day when Spicer finally saw the last one of his works set up—all plugged in and moving as he had once designed—the Cuban government saw him off to the airport with an insistent armed militia guard and a one-way ticket on a night flight to Mexico City. From there, Spicer wired Tamara for enough money to get home.

As Spicer described himself then, he arrived exhausted, defeated, badly sunburned. His deep depression and lack of energy was so intense that he seemed to bring a desolate Caribbean winter drizzle with him into the tiny apartment Tamara had managed to find in her new life as a single mother in New York City. Spicer's mood covered everything over like a tropical sweat that nearly drove his family out of their home. But their troubles were by no means over.

It wasn't long before FBI agents came pounding at the apartment door. They had warrants to seize Spicer's passport and all information he had regarding Cuba. In the months that followed, agents came back at least half a dozen times and, as if placing Spicer under arrest, hauled him off to the Federal Courts building near Wall Street. They sat him down and put a strong light on him, making him explain details of his incredible story over and over again. The agents showed him copies of his signed statement at José Martí airport and accused him of treason. They read evidence from field agent testimony about his many rides around Cuba with government ministers in Russian staff cars. Once, they flashed him spy satellite photos of several of his sculptures and even tried to get him to sign a confession which stated he had engaged in illegal weapons smuggling through clandestine contacts in Sweden.

When none of this FBI harassment yielded results, the Internal Revenue Service was put on his case. During the Johnson and especially the Nixon administrations, leftist sympathizers and activists against the war in Vietnam or on behalf of Cuba were openly and illegally hounded by special agents of the IRS. Spicer was no exception. There were sudden audits. Then seizures of what little property his family had left—an old station wagon, some tools, scrap metal, nothing much. Worse, the IRS put a lien against Tamara's income from her recent job in fashion design consulting she had started working to support the family. All of this was based on fictitious tax bills the figures for which the best attorneys in Manhattan could never figure out. Somehow, the IRS placed a value on all the free steel, plastic and electric motors given to Spicer by the government of Sweden. Once Spicer confessed to presenting the finished results of these materials as what amounted to illegal gifts to the Cuban people, the IRS assigned an outrageously high appraised value to the works, treating them just exactly the same way as if they somehow constituted real income. Finally, an indictment for criminal tax evasion came down from the Justice Department. Spicer was actually handcuffed in front of his children and taken off to jail.

Exhausted, worn down, a broken man by then, Max Spicer pled guilty in a plea bargain arrangement to felony charges of tax evasion and, additionally, he agreed to pay a fine for violating the U.S. embargo restricting trade with Cuba. The deal he made carried no prison time. He was liable for about $20,000 in fines and delinquent tax bills—a considerable amount in '60s dollars that took him ten years of writing quarterly checks until it was finally paid.

There's nothing like financial necessity to drive a creative artist into teaching, as Max Spicer so often said with grim irony on his Cuban nights—as if teaching were a kind of base insult added to all the rest he had suffered. But the truth was—though he would never stoop to admit it in front of his colleagues—he was a born teacher. That's how so many of us remember him, Max Spicer always followed around by an eager coterie of his students through the ice and snow of our campus. More than his students, they were like his congregation, his devotees, his gang—how our college lights kept burning long into the nights as they gathered around him in the drawing and sculpture studios while he shared with them everything he knew. Max Spicer was one of the most popular and outspoken professors we ever had the good luck to have around. Even his violent and explosive temper had its place here, his gifts of sudden rage and profanity combined with the physical menace of his size was more than once a real asset in dealing with the deceptive vagaries of our budget-cutting administrations. In just a few years, Max Spicer raised the funds for and oversaw the construction of a large foundry on our campus—yes, that impressive, tall garage-like building by the old field house is due to him, the high-tech facility in which not only our students but noted artists from all over the world so frequently can be seen in the quasi-religious ceremony of pouring out their immense castings in glowing molten bronze.

And at what a sacrifice, as he in his most darkly private moments with us might confess. In memoriam to Max Spicer's art, we should remember that he essentially quit making sculptures shortly after joining our faculty. Or the few he did manage were quite small—his rule after his experience with Cuba became that no work of his would ever again be larger than what could fit into a suitcase. But whatever the real reason, after Cuba, Spicer turned mainly to drawings, assembling a strange and symbolic collage-form⁄body of work filled with cartoonish Mr. Moon faces, with fish, cows, horses, varying themes of insect-like creatures he said were like the three grasshoppers of the apocalypse decorating many of them. His drawings from this period can be seen hanging all over this campus—the ones in the third floor lounge of the library perhaps the most notable. Most are renderings of two-dimensional figures mechanically arranged among colored scraps of paper, pop culture cut-outs from magazines and newspapers, scattered lines of modern poetry or postmodern fracturings of words written out in his characteristic penciled scrawl in the margins or somewhere in the body of the compositions.

Over the years, the actual size of Spicer drawings also steadily diminished. At first, they were large enough to take up the space of a good-sized wall—made up of a patchwork of smaller pieces to conform to his suitcase sizing rule. After those, there was a series four to six feet on each side. Then his drawings began shrinking in size to the standard dimensions of large sketch pad tablets. Toward the end of his life, when he was more or less in failing health, Spicer worked with the aid of a magnifying loupe doing the most intricate miniature sketches the size of postage stamps, which he would then frame in large white-matted spaces and hang on walls mainly all over his studio and his home.

This progression—or diminishing—of Max Spicer's artistic production might be thought by many to be a sign of failure. But as he often told us, some of his smallest scale work he considered to be among his greatest triumphs, and as a body it was certainly more than enough to satisfy our usually ungenerous tenure and merit committees. Some of his larger drawings were shown at galleries in New York and were written about in reviews. Many of these smaller works are on permanent display in regional museums. His last drawings remain unfinished. They are an incredibly small and detailed series—some no larger than a thumbnail—requiring a mounted magnifying lens over each one so they can be viewed. Several examples of this recent work have been set up here tonight in the dining room. Looking at them again now, we can experience a dizzying yet microscopic plunge into completely rendered landscapes, infinitesimal yet amazing for their painstaking detail, their patterns of exceptionally vivid representative images when properly looked at through the mounted lens. This unfinished series Spicer planned to title *for Kevin*, in memory of his son who drowned.

As for his Cuban works, news of his sculptures was reported to Spicer regularly over the years, mainly by expatriates who happened to visit campus or faculty members who went on research trips, or, in later years, by a few of our Cuban descended students who managed to visit their families still on the island. For almost three decades, Spicer's largest constructions—some might say the most significant work of his artistic life—were reported to be in fine shape, all still functioning kinetically just where he had installed them. Then, of course, as must always happen, history intervened. The Soviet Union collapsed. Cuba lost its vital technical and economic subsidies. It wasn't long afterward that Max Spicer got reports that his sculptures in Cuba were beginning to disappear. First to go were the expensive electric motors that kept many of them moving—ideal replacement parts for Russian-made refrigeration plants. Then it was actual pieces of steel that were missing—high carbon steel that must have found hundreds of good uses all over the island. Finally, Spicer learned third-hand that some of his animal and almost human plastic masks along with his decorative planets, stars and moons could be seen parading around old Havana as parts of costumes of common folk in their pre-Lenten parties at New Year's and Carnival. The day he died, the only of his sculptures left standing in Cuba was the one Fidel Castro himself had seen installed in the courtyard gardens of the National Schools of Art. But no one was sure if it had had its electric motors removed so might be standing there motionless and rusting away. Some of us tried to reassure him of the postmodern conviction that art so appropriated into daily use is surely its highest form of comprehension. He disagreed, sadly. Still, it seemed so uncharacteristic of Spicer that he took this last news with such a spirit of philosophic calm and stoic resignation—so much so that we might conclude this was his eventual stance toward his own mortality.

Last Thursday, Max Spicer was up late in a bedroom he had converted into a small studio. He was hard at work with his magnifying lens on his last intricate miniature drawing. Tamara had just said goodnight and gone to bed. She heard a jarring noise, leapt up and ran out of the bedroom into the hallway. There he was, staggering toward her, calling her name, his face with a strange and terrified expression. She reached him just in time. His heavy weight leaned into her. They collapsed together in the hallway and he died in her arms.

Max Spicer died of a massive stroke. He had been ill with blood pressure problems for a long time, though he and Tamara never let any of us know. It's hard to describe just how much we all will miss him, his large and usually amiable presence, his laughter, his invitations to his Cuban nights. He was vital to our campus life. Our campus life is normally rather sedate, tranquil in its pursuit of the life of the mind, even proud of its ivory towerish isolation in this rural setting with its nearly impenetrable lake-effect snows and ice. Our socializing here outside of offices and the library takes place mainly at each other's homes—these drafty Victorian houses that ring our campus with their images of thought and dignity. For decades, our families have grown close to the Spicer family, our wives have become friends with his. We've watched their three remaining children grow up into mature and sensible adults, becoming friends to our children in ways perhaps only faculty children can on an intimate campus such as ours. These friendships, these fraternal nights spent at each other's homes—these years of deep family experience with each other more than the time spent in classrooms or around the deadly tables of our committees—have come to define all our lives. Our lives will never be the same.

So—the moment has come for us to raise our glasses one last time. To Max Spicer. Yes. And as he himself would finish off his memorable evenings before saying a last goodnight and sending us home—again, to what brought Max Spicer so invaluably here among us for going on thirty-five years, to this obsessive and inspiring idea, this innovative, resourceful energy, this irrepressible spirit of revolution. Yes. One last time. Again. To Cuba.

The Writer's Widow

Not too many years ago, a great writer died. We who were his friends were deeply moved, grieving not only for him but for his widow. She was his second wife, this widow. He married her only two months before he died. There was more than tragedy in this. For such a fine writer to die so young and at the peak of his powers, we were saying. We left the rest unfinished. His good friends, his most devoted readers, we were grieving then and still grieve for ourselves.

That day it happened, some of us hurried to catch last-minute flights, the better known of us making it through the rush of radio and newspaper interviews *in memoriam* to his life. We met at airports. We rented cars. We drove out to the remote town and countryside where the writer had spent his last days. The funeral was held in his beautiful new home overlooking his beloved ocean.

We gathered there over his cancer-ravaged body. He was laid out on a four-poster bed in his living room, in a new suit and tie, in polished shoes. These clothes seemed as strange to some of us as the corpse of a bear dressed that way. We remembered our friend differently, in worn flannel shirts, khaki duck pants, bedroom slippers. Still, this was what his widow wished.

We stood or sat in a large semicircle while she read from her own works—this widow was also a writer—then some of us in turn read words of our own. At times, it seemed the yellowed hairless corpse of our friend would twitch. A foot jumped ever so slightly in the cumbersome shoe. A finger jerked. This was of course from his body naturally adjusting to *rigor mortis*, the recent embalming, as sometimes happened. But still it seemed these small, barely perceptible movements were mysteriously in response to our incantations—that he was really there and in some way listening to this reading for the dead.

Some of the writer's other immediate family were also at the funeral. His ex-wife was there—a tall, dignified woman despite her obvious poverty, which had ruined her teeth. She had once been a high school teacher. Partly because of her recovery from alcoholism—some said also due to the toll taken by the difficult years she had devoted to her ex-husband—she had fallen on such tough circumstances that she had been forced to go back to a hard life as a waitress. This had been her occupation and character during their student days, which the writer had so often used to such good effect in his stories.

The writer's son pushed in close to the body as we were reading. A tall, young, blond version of his father's large and once handsome figure, he reached out and pressed the folded hands in a gesture meant publicly to honor him. Nearby was the daughter, with her shocked blue eyes, her expression of hysteria just barely contained. Most of us knew that the writer had not gotten along well with his children. During his hard-drinking days when success had eluded him, when there was so little money, when chaos and turmoil had ruled his life, the children had taken up their whips, as he used to say. They were wild and troublesome as teenagers, in the full cry of children of alcoholics, which the writer often had said helped to spur him on to so much drinking. Still, in the end, in his last and most productive years, we thought all had been forgiven.

The widow was reading from a long poem, at the foot of her dead husband's bed. She sang her poem in a steady and incantatory style, ethereal, as was her gauzy black dress. Her face was carefully painted, her eyebrows and eyelashes plucked bare in what some thought an affectation *à l'art nouveau*. She wasn't a pretty woman, this widow. But she was strong, solid looking. In the ten years she had known him, as his mistress, she had organized the writer's life and finances in ways he never could have managed himself, freeing him to concentrate fully on his writing, for which his friends were grateful. The widow finished her verses and stepped aside. Morning sunlight shone, suddenly, all over the room.

It was time for the ex-wife to say something, this mother of his children, this first and long-suffering wife, the woman about whom the writer had written so many of his stories. Many of us had known her for decades. We had eaten at her table, been hosted at her writers' parties. We had lived through the very sad time when the marriage had crumbled under the weight of so much alcoholism and poverty. Now this ex-wife faced us, the body of her dead ex-husband behind her, both of them, it seemed, looking out on this last of his many audiences—five or six dozen of us—packed into folding chairs, listening. She drew a long, deep breath. She opened a worn book of stories the writer had written. The book jacket was torn. The binding sagged, exhausted from overuse. She read from the dedication page her ex-husband had written in his own hand. "I loved you first and I'll always love you first," she read. "We've always meant so much to each other and we always will. No one will ever know how much," she recited. She paused in her reading, looking up, significantly, at our faces. Then she closed the book and looked directly at the widow. "No one will ever know," she said.

There are often moments at these sad rituals, funerals at which so many otherwise unrelated and incompatible people are gathered around a death, when everything takes a sudden turn. This was one of those moments. The widow sat rigidly in her folding chair, her face transformed, stunned. Her jaw flinched—as if some hateful word were about to burst with a hiss through clenching teeth.

What followed before the undertaker took charge and we put our friend so uneasily into his coffin was a series of events few of us remember clearly enough that we tell them the same way. Some recall how the ex-wife went upstairs, wanting to take one last look at the writer's study, even to touch his desk, so she might feel somehow closer to him. The widow dispatched her sister, a heavy, squat, solidly built woman, to stand guard with crossed arms at the study door. Was not the ex-wife to be granted a few moments alone in this study, to be private in her grief? Was the widow afraid the ex-wife might actually steal something? "Nothing's to be touched," the widow said. "This is history now."

Other friends recall an hysterical confrontation between the widow and the writer's daughter. This daughter was wild-eyed, pale, frightened. She was a single mother of three young children. Despite her father's world-wide reputation, his years of so much success, his fellowships, his genius grants, his daughter and her children were still struggling to make ends meet on welfare. The writer had needed almost all his money to keep on writing. But he had always stepped in, sending her checks about the third week or so of a month, when the food stamps were running out. The writer's daughter wanted to know something. She wanted her father's widow to tell her now—how was she going to make it without her father's help? Had any arrangements been made to take care of them?

It was hardly the time or place. The writer's widow was indignant at the crassness of such a question at such a time. She retired to her room to prepare herself for the burial. Some of us who had known the writer best took his weeping daughter aside. It was I who clasped her hands and calmed her down by telling her, "Among your father's last words to me, he said, 'Tell the family not to worry. You can trust my wife to do the right thing.'"

The undertaker gave his call. His assistant wheeled the coffin in on its smooth steel carriage that made no more sound than a whisper. The men who were the writer's pall bearers gathered behind a drawn curtain. There was his editor, his writer friends, his widow's brother who had been his fishing buddy, and, of course, the writer's son. We struggled with our friend's large body, so awkward and heavy in death. We strained, lifting him up, what was left of him. One of us slipped with his hold. The writer nearly spilled to the floor.

He lay there, shoulders sideways, legs jutting out, his body half in and half out of his coffin. None of us knew what to do. Not one of us was used to handling corpses. Then the writer's son took charge. He leaned over his father's pitifully yellowed, hairless body. He reached out his arms and took his father around the shoulders in a firm embrace. With great care, with tenderness, he straightened his father out and into the satin cushions. The legs fell into place. The son then pressed his father's cold hands once more and stepped away.

None of this was easy. We knew then, some of us, that nothing would ever be the same again in this world. This was a great writer, after all, some critics already calling him one of the greatest who had ever written. We watched as the coffin lid was quickly closed and fastened. We followed the carriage out to the hearse. Then we moved in to do our grim job. Hard to the handles, we raised aloft our dear friend. We carried him off to his grave.

We left the widow that evening, alone in her grief. Still, she had the comfort of the writer's strong backlist, the three houses, our dead friend's now famous boat, the three cars, one of them a silver Mercedes so often written about which the writer had considered a mark of his finally coming into his fame.

The ex-wife and the writer's children drove away, sadly, in a battered Ford station wagon. By the squealing of the wheels, it had dangerous brakes. The muffler was gone. Both side mirrors were broken off and still hanging to the car by some kind of sprung cables. It was a sorry sight to see. But what could we do? Isn't it often like that? One of his oldest writer friends put it this way, "One gets to leave with all the success. The other gets to stand out in the rain."

The following months were remarkable for the number of national and international events to commemorate the writer's life. The widow traveled, organized, made lists of speakers, chose passages from the writer's stories and poems which would stand in his memory. But curious things began to happen. The lists of literary notables who were chosen to speak often contained people who had hardly known him at all when he was alive. One of the widow's editors, for example, a naturally melancholy man who had perhaps met the writer four times at most, was the keynote speaker for the memorial in New York. And London? The widow's recent

British friends. Only one of the writer's allies from the early days was granted some words. Still, what of it? Who was anyone to complain? This was his widow, after all. Didn't that give her the right to do with him what she wanted?

Then came the first documentary, the biographical film about the writer's life, the one produced in England. The director chose not even to speak to the writer's ex-wife and children, not to mention any of his oldest friends. Rumor was that this director needed the widow's permission—and cooperation— to do the film at all and had been given a list. It seemed almost anyone who had known the writer in the days before he had met the widow was now to be excluded from his filmed history. Why was she doing this? Why was she putting a hand in to revise—the better term might be to select—the telling details about him, now so important to an understanding of his life? One of us, now widely considered a great writer himself, put it this way, "She's treating his life as if he were born the day she met him."

Many of us were relieved when another documentary, produced in this country, didn't cave in to any alleged pressure. The ex-wife, the son, even the writer's mother, were allowed to speak of their memories in front of the cameras.

In the months following our friend's death, we wrote—I wrote—to his widow. Always in the kind, supportive, commemorative and personal style appropriate in letters to widows. One of my letters passed on a polite request from the writer's daughter—she and the widow were no longer on speaking terms—for some help, any financial help at all the widow might manage. The writer's granddaughters were facing a cold winter. They needed shoes. Their stockings had holes in them. Their mother was without the money to buy new coats to replace the ones they had outgrown. It was just that time of year. The writer had always sent a check to help with his granddaughters' school clothes.

Do not write to me or try to telephone me again. I am in grief, the widow answered on a plain postcard.

A new, last book of poems was published. The book represented the writer's final year of dedicated work, in the suffering of his illness, plainly seeing his certain end. Imagine how we awaited this book! What final words, what coded meanings, would his intimate, narrative poetic style contain? Which poems would have personal messages in them for each of us?

The volume was handsomely published, a full-cloth edition. For the writer's friends and rare book collectors, there was even a special, numbered, boxed, deluxe limited edition put out by the editor who had so loved—we might say even worshipped— our dear friend. We opened our books with a melancholy eagerness impossible to describe. But what was this? We found that the writer's widow had written a long introduction, taking credit for the inspiration and some of the actual work of many of the poems and stories our friend had written, and not only in this book, but over the length of his whole career! And when we opened our special editions, under the writer's name on the title page, whose signature did we find?

Some of us gathered where we usually did, at each other's homes, at parties in New York, or at our frequent meetings "on the road," as we say, at campus readings and at conferences. Could it be true, we asked, about the widow's introduction? Was she really responsible for whole stories our friend had written? For revisions of most of his poems? Even, as she claimed, for the ordering of the stories in his most famous collections?

Those of us who had known the writer during his most

productive period scoffed at such a preposterous notion. Our friend had asked many of us for advice on his fiction and poems. More than that, he had taken ideas from out of our mouths, borrowed details we had suggested, had even "stolen" certain lines, with or without permission. Such was the way he worked, the way most of us worked, sharing our creative process. Did that then privilege any of *us* to take credit for his writing?

We began to notice other strangeness. Some of the poems we had known before their collection in the book. Many of us saw them now as slightly changed. Had these lines *really* been there when we had read the poems in manuscript, we asked? Or when we heard our friend recite fragments in progress in front of our fires? And what about our names? Our friend had written many poems in the personal *style journal* characteristic of a now passé vogue in French poetry, often including the names of his friends. What had happened to these names? We couldn't be sure. But some of us were of the opinion that the widow had changed them, cutting out names from the poems then adding new ones of her own choosing.

Not long after this, a respectable literary journal published a manuscript page the widow had submitted. It was a page from one of the writer's most famous stories. A hand not our friend's had circled words, underlined sentences, written in marginal comments. The widow had actually drawn arrows penetrating with her pen our friend's unusually stark, minimalist style, which was in no small measure responsible for his reputation. She was laying claim to it, no less than that. She was unequivocally declaring that the actual grammar and the pace and rhythm of the words were now her own. The widow announced this claim more boldly during a trip to Ireland. She is rumored to have said the famous story was actually her story before an audience of the great writer's Irish admirers. But the literary Irish have never been known to stand on ceremonial courtesies and politeness. The widow was effectively driven off the stage with raised fists and shouts of, "Liar! Liar!"

A few of us kept writing to her, to test an approach to her on these matters, the tone of our letters just barely controlled. No answer.

The writer's ex-wife wrote letters, too, with no response. The ex-wife was suffering terribly. She had nearly died from an abscessed tooth which had been let go too long. Then she was stricken with chest pains, a sure sign of heart trouble. She had to give up her taxing job, the rushing around so many miles each day, serving meals in a harbor fish house. Her old car was no longer running. She was near bankruptcy, in danger of losing her home, all she had left, in a foreclosure. The ex-wife wanted to know. What provisions, if any, *had* the writer made for his family?

She had been with him for twenty-four years. Many of us recognized her at once as the model for the strong, take-charge women which so often populated the writer's stories and poems, his women characters almost always fighting poverty, infidelity and alcoholism. When the divorce came down, just as the writer's first real successes were on the way, his ex-wife had not been demanding. She had not asked for alimony. She wanted no settlement that would in any way hinder the ability of her husband to concentrate fully on his writing. She wanted only for him to write. "Don't worry about me," she had told him. "Just go for it. Do it for all of us."

Ever since, while he was still alive, in an irregular but sure fashion, when he received his book advances or when he sold a story to a premier magazine, the writer would send her long letters of love and gratitude, to which checks were attached. It was never much, the ex-wife said. But the thought was there, and even a small check in the course of such a hard life as hers was treated as a godsend.

With the last money she had in the world, the ex-wife hired a lawyer to do an investigation. From this, she soon discovered a disturbing fact. There had been two wills. The first had been made years before, when the writer was in full possession of his faculties. But it was a very general will, with some unclear language, and it wasn't sure just what his intentions were for his family under the new circumstances. The second will had been drawn up during the last twenty-four hours before the writer died. This was after the cancer had gone to his brain, and when his skin had turned a sickly yellow-green from jaundice, which almost always causes delirium. Just following an emergency procedure which put a drain in his cancer-swollen side, when our friend had been surely on strong pain medications in his last tormented hours, his soon-to-be widow thrust this document into his hands. He signed. He signed this second will and then he died, we might say, so few hours passed between the two actions.

There was a court hearing about the two wills. The first was declared unsuitable. The widow had an array of witnesses for the second will—including her own first ex-husband—all of whom affirmed the writer's clarity of mind concerning this will in the months before his death. The hometown judge ruled in favor of the second will. The widow said, "This is what my husband wanted."

No matter the best advice from some of her dead father's friends that she shouldn't, that her wisest course would be to try to make peace somehow with his widow and appeal to her directly, the writer's daughter got in on these legal actions. She found a law firm to represent her *pro bono* in a suit over an obscure provision of the copyright law—desperate to secure something, anything from her father's estate to see to the security of her children. The widow and the writer's daughter went around in the federal courts about this for years—a terrible bitterness for them both, and a great tragic expense for the writer's widow to pay for her teams of attorneys and seemingly endless briefs and motions, about which she complained in her writing and in lectures as though subjected to some undeserved and tormenting injustice. The irony in all of this is that his widow spent, many of us guess, enough money to send the writer's grandchildren to private school three times over before the case was finally settled. The daughter walked away with some paltry sum—many of us believe it was less in thousands than she could count on her fingers and toes.

As for the widow, the second will was now iron-clad. All rights, income, control of all written and recorded words, all real property, everything the writer had ever done or made in his life or that would ever be made of him and his work now belonged entirely and exclusively to the widow, and to her own heirs for generations.

It's been some years since many of us have had personal words from the writer's widow. She continues on what seems perpetual reading tours. She stands before large audiences, often dressed in gauzy black, in feathered hats with suggestions of veils. She reads in her strange incantatory style from her own works. Then she reads a work by her husband. One of her own, then one of his—as if she no longer wishes anyone to distinguish his voice from hers. And some of us are asking: Is this grief? Is it obsession? Could it be a form of sincere and undying love, trying to keep his voice alive? Or is it all just one more step toward the writer's total and absolute appropriation?

There's something heartbreaking in it all—as heartbreaking as any of the writer's saddest and most wrenching stories. There's a rumor going around that each New Year's Eve, the widow makes reservations at a hometown restaurant where she often used to dine happily with him. She sets the writer's framed photograph at the place across from hers, eats all alone, and, when the time comes, raises a glass to his picture and toasts the new year. How sad this must be! How sorry, sorry this makes us feel for her, no matter what she might have done. And some of us are beginning to ask: What is she doing to her own writing? To her own fine reputation? What is happening to *her* now, even as she seems to persist in rewriting *him*?

As for the writer, new books have followed his death, "authored" by him. Most are composed of smaller works— occasional short essays, reviews, commentaries, even some very early and fledgling stories from his student days. Never mind what the critics are saying, that these ragged, sparse collections only diminish the writer's reputation. And, of course, never mind the widow's by now predictable and self-serving introductions. Some of us, especially those who knew him almost two decades and more and who have read the early work—we can see in these books curious turns of phrase we have a hard time thinking of as his. It's a point about which we will argue from now on. Are there really omitted lines, changed words, canceled phrases which we remember as being there? Or did our friend actually make such revisions in his manuscripts before he died?

The writer's ex-wife has her opinion. She notes that there isn't one compassionate angle, not one generous tone in a sentence, not one kind word toward his first wife or for his children which has been allowed to survive in the new editions.

A collection of fine photographs was also published, which attempts to depict the landscapes and people from which the writer drew for his sources. So many photos of his old friends and family are curiously absent from the book. Of course, many "new" friends, also friends of the widow, are included. When the book of photos was published, there were radio advertisements broadcast in New York. The announcer in the commercial stated in a strong FM news radio voice that this great writer, not so many years ago, "found himself alone and broke in New York, just recovering from alcoholism. He was abandoned by his wife and family. He didn't know where to turn. Then he met—"

An "academic" study has come out, the first of many. On the "chronology" page, there is a date that marks the year the writer "gives up drinking." The date listed is actually *five years after* our friend got sober and never touched a drink again. Those of us who were with him through those desperate, rough times drying out—he was often our homeless guest— and later, when he was first getting well from the disease… Well, we're outraged. This is going too far. How proud our friend was of the years he put in without a drink! The date listed in the study is four years *after* the great writer met the woman who would become his widow. And now the widow has published her own new book—one that some say trades almost exclusively and indecorously on her marriage. On the *also by* page before the title page, the widow lists several books by her husband as though she had actually written them.

The writer's daughter, poor after spending her legal settlement money to pay off back bills and collection agencies, wants to try something of her own to help her and her children's circumstances. She has been working on publishing a collection of her father's letters to her. She's a proud, smart girl, despite her problems, and she deeply loves her father's memory. I've seen some of these letters—filled with kind advice, with long, philosophical journeys the writer took on behalf of his daughter. He is trying to help her learn to live again after being so shattered by the hard life of the writer's family, so much of her childhood spent in poverty. They are valuable letters—insightful, compassionate, lyrical. I count them among the best writing her father ever did. But the letters are not the daughter's property. She is not to publish these letters. Not unless the widow gets to select and make changes, excerpting from them in her by now predictable fashion. And after the bitter court case, the daughter won't see a dime from these letters even if this happens.

Some of us are now resolved. We're hiding our many letters from our friend. We're renting safe deposit boxes. We're finding library archives in which the papers will remain anonymous, locked up for half a century at least. We're putting his papers in places safe from fires, from the hazards of life, and, hopefully, from our greatest fear. I have some manuscripts which the writer and I worked on together, as collaborations—my typescript, his words in ink between the lines. You can bet I'll never let this widow get her hands on them.

The writer's mother died not long ago. The mother, this once hard-working, blue collar woman from the Southern hill country, had a sense of the world passing her by so strongly that she kept moving, six and seven times a year when it was worst, which had always caused her son great concern. She had been too ill to attend her son's funeral—unsettled psychologically is the better way to put it—as she often was during her son's life. She sat out her last years in a small humble apartment, one of the many to which she had been reduced. She watched the broadcasts about her son in which her own name might sometimes appear, but which programs almost never included her. She died in a shabby Medicaid convalescent home, lonely and penniless. It was a place with bad food, as she said, and filled with the chaos and noise of Alzheimer's patients while she was dying.

The last Christmas of her life, the writer's mother sat alone, without money, one box of candy under a skimpy tree, and a mail-order, half a ham the writer's widow had sent to her at the last minute. When we heard about her circumstances, some of us rushed the mother gifts or cards with checks, knowing our friend would never have left his mother in that condition. His mother wept into the phone to her son's ex-wife about her fate, her illness, her terrible poverty. And some of us couldn't help but ask if it really could be—had the widow so abandoned the writer's mother? Left her penniless and alone? Our friend's mother who he would almost never see go a month without a check? It was hard to believe. Among her last words, the writer's mother is said to have awakened out of a kind of coma, crying out, "Where is he? Where's my son?"

The writer's brother—a construction laborer often out of work—carried his mother's ashes almost a thousand miles on his lap, in a Greyhound bus, to the small town where both he and the writer had grown up. He says he had no help from the writer's widow for the expenses of the burial. She sent a modest wreath. Needless to say, she didn't bother to make the trip—a short one for her—to her mother-in-law's funeral.

As for the writer's ex-wife and his daughter, things remain about the same or else they're getting worse. The writer's son left the country to find his way in Europe, perhaps really to get far from the sadness of his mother's and sister's circumstances. They are still scandalously poor and hurt by what has happened. The writer's granddaughters, two of them teenagers by now, are courting the kind of trouble so often bred by welfare and by poverty.

The writer's daughter continues to try, though, as best she can without resources. She finished a college degree. It took her years to do it as a single mother but at least she has a job now and her children off of welfare. But neither she nor her mother has medical insurance. No dental care. The ex-wife and daughter still drive old cars, when such cars are running at all. Food, gas and clothing are hard to afford. But, worse, they have reached a stage when they are reappraising their thoughts and memories of our friend, this writer, the one who used their voices and personalities so often in his stories and poems, the husband and father they once so loved. Under similar conditions, who could not but feel abandoned by him? Who wouldn't ask just what kind of a man he really was, in the end? If the *character* of writers has anything to do with their eventual reputations, will not history one day condemn him for this, for what he has let his widow do?

The writer's books have been best-sellers in Japan, Spain, Germany. They have sold through printing after printing in England, Scandinavia, Latin America. Thousands of copies are studied on American college campuses every year, at almost two dollars each in royalties. The stories have been adapted into plays with sold-out performances in London, New York, San Francisco. His tales have appeared on television. A Hollywood movie was released with great fanfare and publicity, based on a series of his stories, and from which his widow was paid, almost surely, hundreds of thousands of dollars. Currently, there is much talk and excitement about another such movie in the pipeline.

The writer's widow drove his silver Mercedes for years, then traded it in on a new Mercedes. She sold one of the houses for a handsome profit. She divides her time and living space between the other two houses she now owns. And the widow continues to tour the world, endlessly, it seems, trading on the increasing currency of the writer's name, sharing her curious public grief, charging thousands of dollars for her appearances. More books are on the way, "authored" by our friend, more fragments, more unfinished or "discovered" stories to which the widow puts her hand.

Anyone who wishes to make a pilgrimage to the great writer's grave, to that sunny cemetery on the high cliff overlooking his beloved ocean, to the beautiful place where we laid our dear friend to rest that now distant morning of his sad, sad funeral—just go there and see for yourselves. The widow has had a large stone monument erected—mottled black stone, strangely enclosing in its design. Go there. Stand in the black enclosure. Look at what's staring back at you. At the very center of the stone, there's an embossed metal photograph of the widow's face.

Autobiography

Recently, in Las Vegas, a senior citizen from Continuing Education approached me after a fiction workshop. He held open a worn library copy of one of my books—*El Yanqui*, the most forgotten of my out-of-print novels. He was eager to show me some dialogue he had marked on one of its closing pages: "Come on, Harry, let's go. I've got some money, and maybe we can check into the Alton House, you remember staying in that place? It wasn't bad, and maybe the rooms are still only ten bucks a night."

These lines, confronting them once more, seemed unimportant. The man's name was Saul Bromberg, a small, rough-talking New Yorker in his late 70s. He had survived an adventurous youth on the fringes of a world of Jewish and Italian gangsters on the Lower East Side then combat in World War II, also the trauma, from which he had struggled to recover, of being one of the soldiers who liberated Buchenwald, overseeing the burial of emaciated corpses, leading nearby German citizens past the crematoriums to witness their complicity. Saul was writing an earnest autobiographical novel about all of this which had considerable charms despite these horrors.

El Yanqui is also autobiographical. I thought Saul must have a creative reason for pointing out lines from that obscure book. But he said, "Professor... I used to own this hotel, the Alton House. It's been eating at me. Could that have been you and your brother I remember when you were kids?"

He showed me an old business card, grimy at the edges, which had *The Alton House* printed on it, and his name, the hotel's address, phone numbers—offering proof. I stiffened, defensively leaning one hand on the table. I had to will myself to breathe. Grief covered me like the stench of filthy clothes.

Recovering a little, I was able to look into his face. He had a kindly, Jewish grandfather's face, almost comical, with big ears sticking out. His large pitted nose was pushed off center—I knew from his story that it had been punched that way. His face was too thin, an old man's slack gauntness to it that looked unhealthy, slightly bluish. I recalled him mentioning something in class about heart trouble. His face would have been scary, a tough guy's face, an old boxer's face, but it had been softened by age, by his milky hazel eyes squinting good-naturedly through his thick, somehow rabbinical glasses. Those eyes were lit up now with gleefully mischievous discovery. He was onto something and he knew it—uncovering the secret past of another man.

He *had* discovered me—or who I had been years ago—something I had spent much of my life trying to deny and which that orphaned, mostly autobiographical novel never honestly addressed (it might have been a better book if it had). Saul Bromberg was seeing the street kid I was once with my brother Harry. There's a term now—*throwaway kids*—which sums up something of what we were, runaways our parents had quit looking for, hustlers, drug dealers mostly for our own stash, and in the middle of that life I was a sometimes child prostitute, in alleys, in cars, on construction sites, selling cheap feels and hand jobs to pederasts and drunks.

We weren't the only ones. In the '60s, the East and West Villages of New York looked like a ragged carnival of homeless kids and hippies—we called ourselves "freaks"—troops of us milling everywhere. Finding a place to stay was hard. No matter the youth movement idealism promoting togetherness, communes, all power to the people we heard in songs, talked up on the streets, Harry and I learned early on that it was best to keep to ourselves. We sometimes slept in a big cardboard box stuffed with newspapers off 11th by the piers. Or we were part of that roving tribe of addicts and crazies who invaded abandoned buildings in the East Village, ripping each other off, getting high on whatever there was, crashing in any piss-stinking corner we could find. We were always cold. Worse, when we couldn't find a place to sleep, we wandered all night, hanging out in coffee shops until the counter guys kicked us out. We dozed off in the quaking crash and shriek of subway cars or in among the homeless thousands laid out like so many corpses in the tunnels of Penn Station—people just walked by us as if we were already dead—until the cops finally rousted us. They herded us, sleepless and scared, back into the winter streets. Cutting blasts of arctic wind in pure howling misery through the cruel canyons of buildings made us let loose involuntary moans.

When I think of that time, what I see is a picture of this kid with long greasy hair tied with a bandanna like an Apache. He's stumbling along a sidewalk of sharp frozen slush between pools of streetlight darkness, ice like glass shards tearing at the red canvas of his sneakers. He wears an army surplus officer's greatcoat he once thought looked cool but that's way too big and long on him, just wool blanket cloth not nearly enough for that weather, the hem of it dragging in filthy shreds behind feet he can no longer feel. The coat is missing buttons. The kid struggles holding it closed, the strap of a small army surplus gas mask bag slipping off his shoulder so he has to hitch it back up again without letting the coat fly open. The bag holds everything he still owns, everything that hasn't been ripped off—one pair each of dirty socks and jockey shorts, half a roll of toilet paper, a few candy bars, a spiral notebook, tattered paperbacks. He can't stop shivering. His knees are unsteady, his feet slipping and sliding. His brother is just up ahead on the sidewalk. The kid is falling behind—Harry with the back of his navy-blue pea coat silvered in freezing sleet, shoulders hunching over into the sudden face kicks of wind, his guitar case slapping his leg with each long gangly stride. He's not slowing down. The kid is crying, crying out for him to wait up, crying out in rage, crying out to God.

We reached that point when we couldn't take this anymore. We had to find a bed and a hot shower or lie down and die for real. Enough said that the idea of going home—back to our dysfunctional parents, that abusive drunken violence—was far worse in our minds. Any description here would only confirm a sad cliché. Let's leave it that the idea of going home was dreaded more. When being stuck out on the streets got bad enough, there was the Alton House, over on 7th Avenue and 14th, in those days a fringe neighborhood of seedy commercial buildings with a few low-life bars and crumbling tenements and that run-down, dormitory-style hotel now claimed by this same Saul Bromberg standing next to me in my class, in Las Vegas, thirty-five years later, the man who had just handed me his old business card as if our meeting like this were a kind of celebration.

I was trying my best now to be objective again—the teacher—and to understand what he was doing. For the three weeks he had been my student, I had begun to think of Saul Bromberg as a cheerful, beat-up old wise guy who had become like a senior mascot to the other students in my workshop. He always made honest, good-humored comments about stories, even if he was dead wrong in what he was saying. And I had been reading his work and encouraging him (as I always did with seniors who signed up for help with writing fiction) by my tales of Harriet Doerr winning the American Book Award for *Stones for Ibarra* at age 75, of Helen Hooven Santmyer hitting *The New York Times* best-seller list at age 88 with her five-pound opus, *And Ladies of the Club.* And there was my own former student, Sam Halpert, well into his 70s when he put together and published a fairly decent oral biography of Raymond Carver, and who wrote a half dozen fine stories he saw published in the journals (then nothing, and me not wanting to pursue what might have happened to him). In any case, what good would it do to discourage them by the real odds at their age? I pitched writing fiction to these seniors as a self-enriching process worth all the effort for its own sake, art practiced for self-discovery and for the benefit of the soul, like a spiritual quest—let's face it, the standard Humanist reasons to keep the class full enough to justify my paychecks to the head-counting administration. And there were times when I believed that teaching fiction workshops was just one more hustle, only occasionally redeemed by the few genuinely talented writers who turned up, it seemed, by the most unlikely accidents.

So here he was, Saul Bromberg, an older writer not without some talent. But all I saw next to me taunting me with words from my forgotten book was that other man, as I now remembered him with revulsion—the monster at the gates of the Alton House. At the same moment, he was seeing me as I had been then—hungry, terrified, at thirteen already with a hard glazed look of predatory survival from too many nights out there pulling off dicks for money. We were silent for a long time, squared off like this in the classroom, unsure we could believe what we were seeing.

In life and in stories, time and actions seem to me a series of collapsing and expanding frames, something like the internal structures of a bellows. It's as if we live inside the body of an immense accordion, floating in the air, moving through this continually opening and closing machine. We can progress through one of the frames—for some reason, they seem to me triangular in shape, perhaps because of the three-dimensional conceptualization of our sensed world, or of so many religious and psychological trinities, also the geographical calculation from three coordinates to determine any exact location. Imagine: we're pushing our way through this pumping bellows tunnel of dark triangles. We find ourselves at a certain place in the tunnel. One of the frames collapses back, reversing, the bellows closing in on us. Other frames begin to move past or over and around us in the opposite direction. We discover with no little discomfort—that tingling of the mystical or just plain weird— how we've landed in the same place as before, inside the exact same triangle. There's no explanation that fits neatly into our rational world.

The Alton House wasn't a bad cheap hotel, with good heat, clean enough, only ten bucks a night—my going price for a quick hand job and let's hope to get away with not much more. My brother Harry, who could pass for eighteen with a doctored driver's license, was too big and awkward for that hard trade. He waited for me over on 6th, in a Greek coffee shop not all that far from the hotel. I would finish what I had to do. Gangs of us freaky kids would work up by the Holland

Tunnel, catching those supposedly good family men with a taste for boys on the side in their warm cars, stopping off on their way back to Jersey, dangerous because they usually demanded more than I was willing to put out. So I would finish—retching from the gamy smells or worse—then go find Harry at the Greek's and give him the money. More often than not, I was out a few times like this before I found him—one after the other in a numbing, automatic way—so we might put together money to last a week, though it was seldom enough to last that long. Harry pitched in, too, from panhandling and selling nickel bags. Neither of us said a word about where my money came from. That would have been intolerable, breaking the unspoken contract I had made with him but mainly with myself guaranteeing rights to total denial that would one day land me in years of expensive therapy owning up.

Owning up to what? Terror, rage, pain—such inadequate words. Essences, yes, now, for acid and peril half-consciously lived through by looking only to what lay ahead, to that next simple wish. So just forget about it, the car door slamming behind the kid as he hunts for snow or pulls out a wad of coffee shop napkins to wipe off his hand, what good to think about it anyway? The kid is already anxious about the strange tense dance he'll have to go through at the Alton House getting past that nasty little man guarding the doors.

The hotel had a sign by the office we could read through the glass of its battered doors, *No One Under 18 Allowed*. The office didn't have anything like a counter, just a big desk behind a wide open door facing the street. At the desk was the younger face of Saul Bromberg, a face not in any way softened by age. He had thinning dark hair not so bald, fuller cheeks. He kept a plain-end cigarette gripped in his lips, shaping them into a perpetual scowling. He was a hateful presence to me then, small, mean, threatening. I imagined his fist around a bat under the counter just waiting for a kid like me to dare to try and get past him. He was a wiry little man, tough enough he had a reputation for tossing younger men twice his size into the streets (one tale about him was he had once manhandled beefy writer Norman Mailer to the sidewalk in a fury over a bad drug deal, which he in no way tolerated, not in his hotel). There was something biblical about this man under his signs, *No Credit, No Checks*, counting out his change. He was strict with money and house rules, *No Extensions*. We thought of him as pitiless, called him a *kike*, even a *gonef*, for how quick he was known to seize possessions left in rooms if someone didn't pay. We hated the sight of him. We hated him with curses, *motherfucker…*

Imagine: the kid slinking around, shivering in the shadows near the worn steps of the shabby, dormitory-like building. The rooms were all on the floor above. At street level was a dank Irish bar off to one side, down a ways from the hotel doors, a hot stench of sour beer blowing out from a humming fan over its door. On the other side was some kind of deserted garage or something with blacked-out windows. Waiting, how the kid wished that man at the desk would die. It was only him now making him freeze even longer until Harry could sign in, pay cash, and the kid could somehow sneak past him through the doors and upstairs to his only goals—warmth, hot shower, real bed, all it seemed by then he had ever desired. And here he was again, thirty-five years later, this very same man, Saul Bromberg—*him!*

The truth all those years ago was that I never once spoke to him, never met him face to face. I was aware of his hateful presence by legend only and as a moving shape, distantly through the glass doors, lit up in his tiny green office. I was exhausted by then as only people who spend days and nights out on the streets can feel exhaustion—a complete emptying out down to the last feeble threads. I kept well into the shadows outside, out of range of the lone streetlight, praying that this monster at the gates would please go away. I crept furtively to the doors, cupped my hands to the glass, then ducked back quickly down the steps into the darkness, crouching there, scared that man might have seen me. What could be taking so long? Dread like a knifepoint scraped through the lining of my stomach into my spine. I prayed—let the hotel not be full tonight! Don't make us go to the Hotel Greenwich with its cardboard and chickenwire flophouse rooms! Sometimes, this sense of doom fell over me, like the certainty of a beating, that nothing would ever work out, ever, and I was blinded in a wept-out immensity when even suicide seemed no solution because what was the point—it would be like putting out a shadow with darkness. This total blackness covered me when I was convinced for sure we would spend another night out in the cold when it was no longer possible to stand it ten more minutes. Then joy—the rush running through him like a big relaxing bong hit that warmed his blood—he saw Harry's long-legged frame in his navy pea coat moving past the door glass, distantly, vanishing as he started up the stairs. Harry always asked for room number six, at the end of the hall—it was usually available, for some reason—so whenever the kid could sneak in, he would be sure which room.

Then came more torturous waiting, blasts of hellish wind shrieking up the Hudson, ice crystals peppering my face, the pain hurting worse in anticipation of its release. The kid hopped up and down on deadened feet. He closed his eyes and recited like a hippie mantra, prayers and curses spilling through his brain in raw bucketfuls—*please, man, take a break, go away, please, you fucker, when, when, when, ohhhh...man oh man oh man...fuck you, man...please...please...*

The man in the office grew into more than he was, the monstrous shape of everything standing in my way, all the memories of blood and fear of home we carried with us in the streets, all the hateful people I had seen that day passing by not bearing even to look in my direction, all the guys who had felt me over squeezing me in places I didn't want to think about like testing ripe fruit, cheap with their money, greedy when they unzipped, faces like dumb disgusting cows when they shot off, and my rage concentrated then only on him, powered by terror underneath that no one, no one anywhere on this earth, no one would ever *see me*, out there, and finally take me in—take me in without asking anything. Rage rose up from the agony of pure terror. Years later, I would discover this truth in Coleridge, *anger not excluding but taking the Lead of Fear*, the same Coleridge who disparaged novels and said reading them led to *utter destruction of the powers of the mind*. That moment came when I was certain the little man in the office would never let me in. I would be stuck out there forever, could die out there alone. Why the kid was so terrified this would happen, I don't know—Harry would never let more than an hour go by without coming down to find me. Still, the kid was raging, packed full of hate, aiming it all at that man in the office, every passing second murdering him in his thoughts.

It always seemed that man was talking nastily to someone—as if there might be another person with him in the office, out of sight to the side behind him. As the kid stole quick looks, the man's face took on an increasingly gruff, spiteful expression. Could there be somebody with him? Or was this just his way, snarling like that to himself as he leaned over his desk in his relentless smoke, doing his accounts, straightening out our rumpled dollar bills? Minutes passing were small eternities, each a further step into hopelessness. Finally—as always happened—the monster got up from his chair and moved out of view. Shadows hunched up on green office walls. Then mercy—the office door swung closed.

This was my chance. I clutched up the dragging rags of my coat. I flung myself up the stoop and through the doors. I raced past the closed office door. At the end of the hall were stairs and I stumbled up them, two at a time, feet too loud, long coat gathered up like an old woman's skirts. I didn't breathe, certain his voice would shout to stop me. All this took about five seconds. Then I was home free, at the top of the stairs and bounding down the hallway to our room.

"Professor...?"

The floor of the classroom seemed distant. I couldn't exactly feel my shoes in contact with anything solid so I was suddenly unsteady. Ringing started in my ears, a pressure inside my head cutting out all other noise. Saul Bromberg was still pointing at lines of dialogue which had lost all signification, like crude hashmarks, incomprehensible, talking on at me about something I couldn't hear what he was saying. All was buzzing noise. Saul Bromberg's lips were moving, false teeth slipping in sunken cheeks. He was actually happy! He was proud! He was chattering away, all good cheer! It was like a grand reunion, some wonderful surprise! Hail fellow! Well met! Think of it—he was saying—all those years ago, in New York, and now we meet in Las Vegas! And that he should end up my student? Who could calculate such odds?

I had to fight off the urge to reach out and strangle him.

"Professor... Are you all right?"

Paradise was that tiny room—number six at the end of the hall. Harry would already have his wet filthy clothes off down to his underwear, ready to head out with his clean towel to the shower down the hall and be first to climb under the blankets, between clean sheets, of the single bed we both fit ourselves into with minimal grumblings and a few sharp elbows to the ribs. He usually waited until I was safe in the room before he took his shower. The first thing I did even before taking off my coat was to wrap my arms around the radiator that stood against the wall. It was painted gold. I let it burn. I knelt there, hugging the gold radiator, burning, listening to it clicking with steam. Only later, late enough that I stood least chance of being seen, would I sneak out to the shower, that miracle, the hot water, the disinfectant-smelling steam—soaping and scrubbing, scrubbing and soaping, hands first, always my hands five times at least, like a superstition, before I would let them touch any other part of my body.

Saul Bromberg pushed closer to me in the ugly yellow classroom, his look changing. He grabbed insistently at the sleeve of my tweed jacket. This student was actually putting his hands on me, leaning into the pure revulsion for him I could no longer hide. Saul was talking to me, close to my ear now, demanding that I listen. That weird sense which I can only describe as being in two places at once—or of being two people at the same time—suddenly woke me up enough to hear him.

"Professor... I'm... I'm sorry," he stammered. "The way we had to be. You know the way you kids were, the way you lived. Let one of you in and let the others see... We'd be overrun! But Sylvia—that's my wife—Sylvia would always say, 'Saul, don't leave that boy out there! It's cold! Go out and get him!' But you know the kind of neighborhood it was! We couldn't let grown men check in with boys! We didn't run that kind of place! You get what I'm saying?"

"Yes," I said tautly. "I understand."

These words were automatic. I understood nothing.

"No, you don't understand," he said. "It's bothered me for years. Sylvia—that's my wife—she looked for you, four and five nights a week. Remember? How you didn't leave the room for days?"

I shook my head. I had no memory of a woman there. But come to think of it, whole periods of dreamlike time passed in that tiny room at the Alton House, my brother out with his guitar panhandling and bringing up food and bags of pot, the both of us sitting on the floor, cutting a big bag of fragrant green flowers and leaves into dozens of little nickel bags he would go out and sell, nights hanging out in front of the music bars and cafes of West 4th Street, Bleeker and MacDougal—that hippie carnival scene. I would wait for him in our room, sitting on the bed, happy and warm—overjoyed— or huddling on the floor next to the radiator writing down everything I had experienced or thought on the streets in spiral notebooks I would later, with solemn intention, bury deep in city trash baskets so they could never be ripped off and read by anybody.

Long dreamy days, I would lie back in bed reading paperbacks bought for a dime or up to a quarter apiece out of the bins on 8th Street. Books I can recall from those days are Allen Ginsberg's *Howl and Other Poems*, Lawrence Ferlinghetti's *A Coney Island of the Mind*, generous doses of Jack Kerouac's *The Dharma Bums* and *Big Sur* along with *Junkie* by William S. Burroughs. Eugene Ionesco's *The Bald Soprano* was in there, too—I can remember reading that crazy dialogue aloud, to myself. Mixed in with these were Robert Heinlein's *Stranger in a Strange Land, The Foundation Trilogy* by Isaac Asimov, all of Ray Bradbury—everything we considered cool and for sale in the bins, most of it possible to read while very stoned. (I still catch myself thinking of the so-called 'beat generation' and science fiction as more or less the same thing.) A whole week could pass by this way like one warm day. Mid-mornings, when only a decrepit old cleaning lady was around and this young guy snoozing at the desk downstairs—both seemed to speak only Russian—I would leave our room, run quickly over to stores on 8th, then back to hunker in again before Saul Bromberg, the owner, came on shift around noon. Or if I went somewhere to hang out longer, like over to the hippie scene on West 4th or St. Mark's Place—like over to the Eastside Bookstore—I would have to wait for night when I could sneak in again. And so our time passed, much of it like this hazy stoned dream, until we ran out of money.

"Why don't you just go home!" Harry would say then, frustrated, ready to start crying, holding himself back from punching me. "Why are you following me around? What are you *doing* here! Do you know what the *fuck* you're *doing*?"

He blamed himself. He had tried jobs under the table— bagging incense at a head shop, washing dishes, unloading trucks—so I wouldn't go out and do what he wasn't saying we both knew I would soon be doing. But he also understood how many times I had tried—we both had tried—home, as he had called it, and that cycling abusive certainty that we would be driven to run away again, back to living this same reality.

"The two brothers, Sylvia called you," Saul Bromberg was saying. "She wanted me to call shelters or the police but I talked her out of it. What would they send you back to? I knew. Believe me, I *knew*... It got so she made me leave room number six open until last, the one your brother always asked for. Nights you didn't show, 'Wonder where the kid is, and his brother,' she would ask. That went on about two years.... Remember? Two winters?..."

There are holes in my memory about that time, these buzzing blank spaces filled with noise like destroyed recording tapes, big gaps when I've tried to write down in the therapy workbooks—they call them "Life Healing Histories"— just where I was and what I was doing. It's typical of a condition my therapists refer to as *dissociation*. I've never had much desire to explore into this history very far with them, no matter what they say. They tell me there's a price to pay for this avoidance—nightmares, sure, but worse, an inability to experience true intimacy, friendship, love. So they keep trying.

"When your brother checked in, we couldn't leave you in the cold," Saul Bromberg said. "But how could we let you in without breaking rules? You were brothers! You weren't hustling in our place! We finally settled on shutting the door to the office. Remember? How you used to sneak in? Run up the stairs? We always made sure we heard you safe in the room until we opened the door again. We waited for the night-shift guy, told him, then went home. Sylvia slept better knowing you were there," he said. He said this with real sadness, liquid eyes behind his glasses. "One day, you two were just gone. But we always wondered. That's the way it was in the hotel business. People came and went," he said, a catch in his voice.

He must have known from reading *El Yanqui* that my brother Harry was busted then drafted and sent to Vietnam, from which he came back one-hundred percent disabled. He also knew that I had been saved—caring teachers during another violent cycle back home improbably picked me as a foreign exchange student to get me out of there. I was sent to Argentina—what happened in that country the main story of my autobiographical novel. I was more or less adopted by my host family, who somehow understood. They were sensible, kind parents. Even during tumultuous political events in their country, the opening actions of a story of tragic violence and murder by state terrorism which would later overwhelm them, they provided me with a real home, an education in a private school, money, clothes, new brothers— a house full of art and books and love. This had been enough to change a life.

I thought he might say something more but he didn't. He stood there, sentimental, waiting for me to answer him, nostalgic for something I never knew I had shared. At a perilous time in the kid's life, with the kid convinced he was doing just the opposite, he had actually been one person in the world who did *see me*, as I had wanted so desperately to be seen. He had done all he could within his set of harsh rules to take me in— what the kid had wished for, prayed for, from another human being. Saul Bromberg was a soft, giving presence now in my classroom, a true *mensch*, a caring old guy whose wisecracks and anecdotes made him beloved among his fellow students— really just this sweet old man standing there with one of my books, asking something from me.

The feeling we shared then was really something. It reached into the literary we had bonded over in my office—the Aleph of Borges with its glimpse of the infinite, the voice of Whitman that is the universe, Rilke's terrifying angels. It felt like levitation. Suddenly, all of us—these four characters—landed in exactly the same triangle in the bellows. Our stories became the same story. We asked each other for forgiveness.

Matisse

One evening, I was just back home from a trip to Washington, D.C., talking happily and too much about the East Wing of the National Gallery and its exhibition of modern and contemporary art—works by Mark Rothko and Robert Rauschenberg, Willem de Kooning and Anselm Kiefer, Alexander Calder and Nancy Graves—some of the best of everything. I described the architecture of the building designed by I.M. Pei, its expansive lobby, how entering into that lofty spectacle of airy light invites new self-definitions. "And above all the rest, in a special room like a castle tower, there's only Matisse," I said.

A long moment passed, my brother Harry thinking this over, distracted from the quick flashing images on his muted TV. "The folks always had such bad taste," he finally said. "Cowboy art. Cheap bronze horses, wood carvings of old Indians. That Norman Rockwell coffee table book somebody gave them the year the Christmas tree went through the window. No taste," he said.

It was unusual he would mention our parents. Both were alcoholics, and physical abusers. We spent years of our youth running away, had suffered together as homeless runaways because of them. Since my marriage broke apart, we had been sharing a house in Las Vegas, going on six years, and we almost never mentioned our parents, that past that deserved no mention as far as I was concerned. Stranger still was his reference to that Christmas, the traumatic family memory of our old man wrestling our mother to the floor, a butcher knife aimed at his chest. Colorful shards of busted Christmas bulbs sparkled everywhere. Trails of wind-blown tinsel hung from quivering scythes of glass, all that remained of the picture window in the living room after our father had tossed the tree through it—that sad dark thing crushed, on its side, in the muddy front yard. Later, by way of apology, he said, "Just call it a bad day, kids. Ho-ho-ho."

"So, what... What are you *saying*?" I asked my brother.

"Makes you wonder how it is we found art," Harry said. And that was all he was going to say. He picked up the remote and flicked off the TV. He got up off his couch and strode out—the garage area of our home had been reconstructed into his private apartment—his time now, as at ten every night, to go to bed.

He left me frustrated, feelings of homecoming shot down. Who was he to judge? What the hell did *he* know about art? As far as I could recall, my brother had never even stepped foot inside an art museum. He collected impressionist calendars, going back ten years or so by now, and he had some mounted posters on his walls, one of Monet's lily pond series in dreamy purples and greens, Van Gogh's austere bedroom at Arles with its vivid primary colors, the American flag by Jasper Johns. I intuited from these that he meant some identification with the romantic myth of the rebellious artist, the misunderstood genius, solitary and in constant flight from a society unable to accept him. Ever since his tour in Vietnam, his disability checks from the VA had privileged this attitude of alienated disaffection with a hateful world. He had spent ten hours a day for the last thirty years watching television. When had he ever taken time or effort and "found" art? And what did our rotten parents have to do with this anyway?

Later that night, unable to sleep, these questions turned inward. This started with a mental inventory of the art on my walls. Featured are a series of six postmodern drawings by Jack Nelson, a lesser-known artist from the once trendy Krasner gallery, Julian Levy group, which I had been collecting. I was also proud of a cartoonish lithograph of a spaceman-like figure in tones of red by the Mexican master, Rufino Tamayo, and of another, a black-and-white linoleum cut, like one of M.C. Escher's stark labyrinths only more haunting and grotesque, by Benavídez Bedoya, the bohemian Argentine. All these were arranged neatly on the living room walls, at the same precise, eye-level height. Over the staircase hung a primitive *indio* tapestry of a pre-Columbian deity, a stark face inside a corona of serpents; in the dining room, a salmon god print by Pacific Northwest Indians; in the hallway, a pleasant watercolor seascape picked up in northern Spain and a Currier & Ives that in no way went with anything else. Off in bedrooms were some colorful street artist drawings and two reproductions from museums—Chagall's magical rooster, J. Solana's *tertulia* group portrait of well-dressed, learned Spanish men. There was nothing of any special financial value. Still, I liked what there was and knew why each piece was there. The fact that I was fortunate enough I could own a house—even have walls to hang art on—was never far from my thoughts. But what did any of this really say about taste except what I could afford? When and how had I ever *found art*, if that was even the right expression? What could the discovery of art mean to a life?

Memories rose up in colored bits. The night was blue. Shadows were like sharp blue cut-outs on fresh white snow. Fallon—Michael Fallon, a sometimes chickenhawk like me, from Boston, I took up with after Harry was busted then drafted and shipped off to basic training—Fallon waited around the corner, in an alley, off a little side-street meeting Berkeley Street. He was there, ready with his club. It was a good club, a heavy stick, maple, maybe, like an old lathed table leg but not too heavy. We had wrapped it with a few rags at one end so it wouldn't cut so easy. We didn't want any blood. One sharp crack on the head to get his attention, like Fallon said, and make him give it up. We didn't want to kill anybody.

The trick was not to let his head hit the pavement, I was thinking, the guy's arm greedy over my shoulders like he owned me, like I was his boy now, waiting for me to do him in the alley. He was drunk, his sour breath coming out one side of his mouth in quick white puffs, squeezing me to him around my shoulders, not in any tough way, almost a fatherly way, protective, kind of—this older guy with a red, cold-burned face, like a face from a painting by George Grosz in its self-absorbed, urban quality, sharp nose in the air, striped red tie, glasses, hair dyed the color of a new blond broom.

His name was Howard. Of all the guys I once sold myself to, his name I still remember. He wasn't a bad guy, just drunk, lonely, happy enough a boy like me was available. I had done him once before, last week, around the corner in the same alley. He'd picked me up on Columbus and walked me over, through angled residential streets of the South End, meaning to take me to his car. Boston was confusing to me, streets running every which way, narrow streets—the low brick apartment buildings and townhouses felt like they leaned over my shoulders. I told him I was scared to do it in his car. I'd had a bad experience in a car. Not long before, in New York, a guy in a car slapped me so hard he busted my eardrum, then he forced my head into his lap. It took weeks before that plugged up sensation that drove me crazy went away, the painful muffled drumbeats of my voice like talking underwater. When he heard this, Howard was ready to say no, maybe we should better not, all guilty, hunching down into his coat collar, a soft blue cashmere coat that felt like real money. But I said why not, he wasn't that kind of guy, and how much I needed the ten bucks. Then all that happened was me unzipping him in the alley, jerking him off while letting him feel me up until he came, a few weak dribbles in my hand.

He gave me a twenty. He let me see how much he carried in his wallet. That was his mistake. And I was already saying I was sorry, I could do a lot better for him, but he said that was just fine, dear, thank you, maybe next time. I read him for one of those "A-list" fags. They actually had lists for themselves, ratings for how classy they were, like everybody seemed to be rated for class back then in Boston. His other mistake was letting me know where he hung out, in one of those upscale, "discreet" private clubs just off Berkeley, a place with smoke-tinted bay windows reflecting faint glimmers of candlelight—chiaroscuro with a few strokes of orange from a fireplace. Older, well-dressed men gathered around polished colonial tables like some kind of grandfathers' club, sipping drinks around a piano bar. He really wasn't such a bad guy, this Howard, very effeminate, as soft and nurturing as a woman. He would have let me get away with doing nothing for him and would have paid me the same. Still, it was his fault. He should have known.

Committing a crime isn't so much the actual doing of it as the setting out to do it—that decision, hours or days before, when events become inevitable. This is especially so when the crime involves more than one perpetrator and the solemn step of actually injuring somebody, a conspiracy, two or more criminals now interdependent, set on their deal. Backing out is like a loss of manhood. What I might have done on my own was different—I understood this even then—already sick, my stomach twisting around itself like wringing out sour pickle juice, every part of me wanting to turn this guy Howard in the other direction and push him away. I wanted to shout at him—it took will not to shout—*Look where you are, man! Nobody's on this street! Look around! Are you stupid or what?*

But what kind of "brother" would I be then to Fallon? He depended on me. He had set me up in Boston as I had never been set up anywhere, with college girls from B.U.—Kathy and Dee—in their cool, trashy apartment near Kenmore Square. This was pretty amazing in itself, since Fallon was a stick-skinny guy with a shaved head—he had just done this down in New York after getting lice—about as uncool looking as anyone could imagine in those days of Beatle haircuts, his teeth black at the gums when he smiled. When I think of Fallon, what I see is a study in grays, tattered clothes washed out to the same dirty shade, body just a gray picket fence of bones hung with sickly colorless skin, his eyes set deeply into circles like messy pencil smudges. We were both geeky-looking kids, little more than fifteen, and these girls were *in college*, man, living in their own apartment, with all the equipment, stereos, rock star posters on the walls, orange juice in the refrigerator, lots of clean towels, a car, everything, way out of our league. The deal was that we would get them their drugs, pot and pills, mostly, enough for them and to supply their student friends. These girls liked speed—pills called "Black Beauties" and these other green and white capsules known as

"Christmas Trees." Fallon had connections for pharmaceuticals, and I had brought a small shoulder bag full of Mexican green up to Boston.

November was like one endless college party. We crashed on the living room floor in their place, warm and settled into sleeping bags they gave us, Fallon and me facing each other over a short space of carpet that smelled like patchouli and old spilled wine, big shared ashtray within easy reach. We had really scored. That was how it started, anyway, before Fallon managed one crazy drunk night to get Kathy pregnant.

Kathy was the heavier one, a little dumpy, even, with a body like a fleshy Rubens and a classical face—a face that might have come off a wall mosaic at Pompey, if her nose had been a little straighter—natural dark curls, a greenish tone to her flawless skin. Dee was the prettier one, with sandy hair and freckles, a leggy body she covered up with over-sized army fatigues, a fad for college girls then, and she had this way of reclining, languidly stoned on the couch, one long arm cocked behind her head in a pose like a sensual Modigliani. The semester let out. Kathy and Dee went home on vacation, leaving us their keys, the whole issue of how to deal with Kathy getting knocked up resolved with tearful dramatic scenes over too much wine at their kitchen table that she would go down to New York after New Year's to get an abortion. Abortion, still illegal in Massachusetts in those days, as in most of the country, had only recently opened up in New York, and it could be arranged for five hundred dollars.

Five hundred dollars. After the girls left on break, Fallon and I got by on what were called "garbage eaters"—hanging out at a place called Sizzleboard on Kenmore Square, finishing off half-eaten burgers and fries left on peoples' trays. We sat around street corners, Fallon bumming my cigarettes, drooping his gray shaved head between his knees, cursing his luck, obsessed with the idea that he had to get up five hundred dollars to take care of "my girl," as he kept calling her. I understood his emphasis, as if having any kind of girl was proof he wasn't turning into a fag, our greatest unspoken fear doing for money what we were sometimes doing. "My girl needs five hundred bucks. Five hundred bucks," he said. He reached his gray clothespin fingers into my jacket pocket for another of my cigarettes, the last one, crumpling my empty pack and tossing it away.

Fallon partly grew up in Roxbury, until his mother had been declared unfit and sent to jail for shooting smack. He kept running away from foster homes in Boston down to Providence then to New York to get away from people who were looking for him. That's where I had met him, in the East Village street scene. Fallon had been baptized a Catholic and actually wanted Kathy to have the kid. Second best was at least he could pay for the abortion, like taking the sin onto himself. He was planning to go with Kathy to New York, hold her hand, wait outside the medical office. He even had fantasies of getting her to drop out of school and hitch with him to Colorado, to some place in the mountains where he had friends. He was crazy. It didn't do any good to tell him five hundred was like nothing to this girl, her parents lived in Connecticut and were shelling out thousands for college. And it did even less good to tell him that it wouldn't be long before this girl would have nothing more to do with him. These were the kind of college girls who lived in furnished souls, who had Cape Cod minds, swingsets and lawnmowers in their genes. Whatever it was they were doing with us was just their way of slumming, a mistake from which they would soon wise up. Nothing I said changed anything. "Five hundred bucks," he kept saying. "Five hundred beans…"

The club—our stick—came down on Howard's head with a sickening sound of wet rags, *sssplap!*—like wet plaster on a wall. It was something felt as a disturbance in the air more than heard, like the whizzing of a baseball bat striking out. Howard staggered and started going down, his slick coat slipping in my arms, still, I managed to break his fall, letting his weight lean into me, and I turned him around as he was falling, lowering him down on his side, heavily, against the brick wall of the building. He lay there, not moving. Little splashes of blood appeared near his head, in the snow, like black paint splatters in the blue shadows. It was up to me to reach in under his expensive coat, in under his gray tweed jacket, lean down close into his lemon after-shave scent and feel—at least he was breathing—for his wallet. He was just coming to about then, eyes blinking and confused, his horn-rims flown away. His shoes started to kick against the building. He groped one arm up, blindly, fingers closing on a handful of my hair. I yanked my head back. My hair ripped free. We had planned to take out the money and leave him the rest, save him the hassle of losing his I.D., but we were already running up the alley, then along the street, fast, sliding through each turn with that high squealing laughter that comes from tension letting loose, our footprints making tracks like pallet knife splotches in the fresh snow. We must have kept running all the way to Commonwealth before we dared slow down. We tossed the empty wallet and our stick in a trash can somewhere on the way.

Later that night, we got drunk on cheap sweet wine in the girls' apartment, listening to their albums, not looking much at each other but when we did saying only, bitterly, "That faggot," and laughing, forcing it out—deep with self-hate— until there was no longer any feeling.

With money from the wallet, and selling off some stereo speakers Fallon lifted out of an elegant store display right in front of everybody, running for gray daylight with one big speaker balanced over each shoulder, we put together the five hundred he needed. The girls came back for New Year's, as planned, for a party at one of their rich girlfriends' houses in the wealthy hills outside the city. It was also to be Kathy's send-off party before her trip to New York, something she didn't want to talk of or even think about now. She and Fallon were hanging all over each other the whole time. I have this image of him sitting in her fleshy lap, a ragged, starveling boy holding a jade pipe up to her lips. Dee was disgusted, suggesting—with a yellow sneer—that we should make our plans to be out of there when the semester started. She threw a fit at me when she found out I had been sleeping in her bed, even though I had washed the sheets and made it up as neatly as in any hotel.

Of course, Fallon and I were still invited to the New Year's party to supply the drugs, though it was pretty clear by then there was little reason for me to be hanging out now, since Fallon could have managed everything himself and Dee couldn't stand the sight of me. And I was ready to move on. As the cold, shut-in days had passed over that Christmas break, including a lonely Christmas day spent drinking wine and smoking pot in front of the TV, Fallon and I playing too cool with each other to observe any ceremony, we had started getting on each other's nerves. Ever since the mugging, we were as careful as cats around each other, not saying much, eating on different schedules, stepping cagily aside when we passed each other in the hall on the way to the bathroom. It was hard to believe we had been like brothers down in New York, watching out for each other in the cars, up near the

Holland tunnel, working commuters into Jersey. We spent a lot of time shut off on our own in the girls' rooms, Fallon's voice echoing faintly but almost constantly from down the hall, using Kathy's phone way too much, long distance, to her and to his friends in Colorado. I was holed up not wanting to share my few packs of hoarded cigarettes, lying in Dee's bed that smelled faintly like perfume and sweet peppers—a fresh, young girl smell. I went through her things, her drawers packed full of silky, lacy underthings, all the pockets and purses in her closet full of clothes, collecting loose change, hairclips, pills. She had bricks and boards loaded with books, mostly textbooks, and I remember working my way through *Modern Principles of Biology,* staring long hours into vivid color plate diagrams of the chemistry of life, the double-helix, unicellular organisms, reproductive systems, human anatomy, because I suddenly missed an education and this seemed like something I should know. I've talked since with my therapist about this time. She makes me be objective about it—see not *me,* but *the boy, the kid*—always asking, what about that *kid*? What about *him*? What was *he* feeling?

The boy was lying half-naked on a bed in a tangle of sheets, dressed in a girl's silky, florid pink robe, waiting for his only set of clothes to finish drying. His hair was long, straight, dark auburn, falling to his shoulders like a girl's. He had this glassy, almost evil look, a gleam of decadence like the boys in Caravaggio. He was smoking, sitting propped against the wall, a heavy volume of biology text balanced in his lap, winter gray light falling in a rectangular column through a nearby window. Out the window was an alley, with shapes of rusty fire escapes, in deep perspective off below these dark lines a wet gray wooden fence falling to ruins—it was the back of what used to be the old Boston Circus rock concert space, black and white posters from some long ago performance advertising *Procol Harem* stretching out, along with others faded beyond all color or recognition, one after the other in an uneven continuous row on the tilting cockeyed fence until distance dissolved into hazy grayness.

The boy was staring out the window, thinking over his life, which had its own rules, its boundaries and codes he was still learning. He was giving hand jobs, sometimes doing more— he had to admit this to himself—they paid twenty, up to thirty bucks, and it wasn't so bad, not really, once he got over the initial gag response, no worse than seawater with a dash of Clorox bleach, get it over with, quick, then forget about it, only it was getting harder to forget. He was aware that he was gradually giving up every moral value he might ever have possessed. And he knew it wouldn't be long before, like Fallon, he was taking it up the ass. What else could he do? Paper routes? And even if he could get the money together, who was going to rent him a place? What would turning up at any of the shelters do for him but get him a one-way trip with a social worker back to that same chaotic house—to the old man and old lady—from which he kept running away? Worse, he saw himself headed with certainty in the direction he had almost gone already, that night with Fallon, how one day, soon, it would happen—he would help a killer kill. He saw again that picture of Howard, how they had left him bleeding in the alley. And he was suddenly scared, fear like little jumps under his skin. A feeling of doom overwhelmed him, a physical sensation like some limitless black space opening up inside into which his body, his strangling voice, his hopes, were endlessly falling. Most likely, it was already too late. The cops were probably looking for Fallon from the stereo rip-off. What if they caught him, made him roll on the other thing? *I'm not like him*, he was thinking. *I'm not a criminal. My only mistake might be sticking around too long...*

The reality struck him that this—a warm bed on a cold winter afternoon—this was the best it might ever get. He thought again of home, going back to that house full of violence, the old lady shutting herself in the bathroom threatening suicide until the old man kicked the door off its hinges; being slapped awake in the middle of the night, made to stand at attention, yelled at for nothing he understood in the heavy boozy blasts of their unhappiness; the times the old man had loaded his revolver and waved it around, the kid screaming at him to stop, until he pointed it at the kid then at his own head and told the kid to just say the word, *say it*, he said, *go ahead, say the word.* He recalled the nights of dishes smashing, slaps, screams, their beating each other, tormenting and threatening their children, and, after all of this, the boy having to try and sit in school through classes with kids younger than he was by now—he had started eighth grade three times by then—kids who were like cruel strangers and he felt like the only fool. There were good reasons he and Harry had run away—the oldest of seven, so first able to run, though most of the rest would be gone by the time they turned fifteen, too. Years later, talking over our father's guns, my therapist asked me how many times he had shot one off in the house. It took a while, counting in my head, in successive jolts. "Never at us. He never shot at people. The walls, a glass lamp, the ceiling in the family room. We used to dig the slugs out. We carried them in our pockets, like charms. Or like the opposite of charms. You'd think somebody'd call the cops but nobody did. The neighbors wanted nothing to do with it, they acted like they didn't hear a thing. He shot the shit out of the dishwasher when he couldn't fix it. Some nights, he set down a bottle of bourbon and his pistol next to it on the coffee table. He left them there, like equal threats, while he lay on the couch and us kids sat around watching TV like we were a normal family. Then her suitcase. Her suitcase that time she tried to leave him," I said, counting back. "Eleven," I finally said. "Eleven times."

New Year's Eve, we all rode together in Kathy's station wagon filled with her friends—three other guys, also students at B.U., and four or five girls picked up on the way, all of us crammed into every available space in the car, my job to sit hunched over way in back keeping the pipe loaded and passed around. I'm not sure in which direction we went into the snow-dusted hills, on narrow country roads, ever bigger houses more distantly lit up behind high iron fences, land-scapes of black, bare, twisting trees. We finally spilled out at a modern, spread out, split-level house at the end of a short lane, big and lush enough, but not at all the huge colonial mansion I had been imagining. Music sounded from inside as a girl opened the front door, welcoming us in with the latest release from the Beatles, *the magical mystery tour is coming to take you away....*

The girl in the door was a daughter of a famous Boston family. They had the name "Kennedy" as their middle name. This was how she and all in her family were introduced, with emphasis, "_____ *Kennedy* _____." Her name's left blank to spare her possible embarrassment. Who hasn't done things they would rather not own up to in their youth? While her parents were away, Fallon and I supplied her party with two dozen hits of acid, pills of many descriptions, and what was left of my marijuana—enough these days to send us to prison for ten years. She was an attentive, generous hostess, taking time and effort to make sure each of us was settled with drinks in cut glasses, catered food on gold-rimmed Limoge plates, all welcomed comfortably into her home. There were only about twenty people there, special guests she had considered for this drug party, selected as appropriate company for getting high with, laughing with, tripping with, and, in that era when so-called "free love" was just becoming fashionable, most guests finally getting naked and having sex, so some trading partners with in candlelit rooms. The atmosphere was giddy with uninhibited release, music by the Stones and the Beatles and the Butterfield Blues Band whipping up the energy, half-naked bodies flashing through into the living room from time to time for more pills, more pot, taking breaks, lounging on pillows in the corners, refilling their glasses with vintage wines.

Fallon was quickly pulled off down a hallway by Kathy, as happy as I'd ever seen him—hoping his hopes, knowing his luck was too unlucky to last but laughing all the harder for it, high enough just on this night, kissing her two faces with boyish tenderness. They vanished, leaving me at the coffee table near the main stereo, surrounded by plush deep sofas, laying out drugs in little piles—*uppers, downers, LSD*—like at some central filling station, cautioning everybody not to take more than two of any one thing. Why this suddenly became my job, I don't know, except that I was feeling strangely uncomfortable, out of place, as I later learned was always true when I found myself among the rich, unable to hide how conflicted I was with both envy and contempt, and I was scared that our hostess would unmask me, discover what I truly was and kick me out unless I could impress her as useful. To this day, I have to fight this conflicted response—the choice of either falling all over myself to impress wealthy hosts or heading straight to their kitchens to load up on food and booze, then escape with it all out the back way. That night, this feeling wasn't justified by our famous hostess. She couldn't have been more gracious. Later, she found me all alone in the living room, up some steps of the split-level from the more crowded family room, taking a break from the loud music, and she asked me, while tying her silk kimono closed, warmly high, with firelit eyes—she was like a beautiful odalisque in an oriental dream—if I was sure I had had enough food.

Someone called her name. She reached out and stroked the boy's long hair, fondly. She left him alone in her living room, every part of it draped with wealth. The kid was clear in his mind, not stoned in any way by then, someone had to keep count of the pills, keep track of who had taken what, no cops and ambulances needed, please. Then this terrible feeling of being out of place hit him again, as if he didn't deserve even the air he breathed in this house. He had the sense that his even sitting on such rich furniture as this might soil it forever. He was miserable, isolated from the others, the thought striking home that not one of the girls had so much as glanced in his direction, not even once, with anything like desire. And he had been too shy, strangely, to make any kind of sexual move when it might have counted.

What he did, finally, was get up and wander around that house. This wasn't any willed wandering but more gradual than that, mysteriously drawn up to his feet—pulled out of his own small life—captured then visually following, one after the other, as if each were speaking to him with a secret voice, the pictures hanging on the walls.

That house was his first museum. Over the mantle of a square brick fireplace was a splash of brown, then yellow, then green, earth-toned fruits, purple standing jar, the center of the canvas filled with masterful swirling brush strokes creating multi-colored flowers radiating light. Years later—though it was only a skillful reproduction of the original on loan to museums—I would realize it was a still life by Cézanne. On the wall opposite, rectangle blocks of solid colors on a white background—Piet Mondrian. Down the hall hung a lithograph in minimal black lines, mounted in a plain black frame, showing satyrs and the Minotaur dancing, circling in a mythic space, ecstatic and wild, that characteristic signature at their feet, Picasso. In a corner, smooth standing marble white as salt tapering to a thin stem in the middle then taking on mass again, mounting upward in a pure symmetry, suddenly rising as if leaping up from sky—how much he wanted to touch it but was afraid—a Brancusi. Along off-white walls leading toward the open blue space of the kitchen were a series of three small prints of funny cartoonish shapes, sticks, circles, half-moons, squiggles, like painted tinker toys, here and everywhere in them eyes looking out, eyes looking straight *at him* from constellations full of joy—Joan Miró.

There were other, more romantic and colonial pictures in the library. Was that a seascape after Homer? Were the learned men all gathered in a great teaching hall by the bookcase a genuine Eakins? There were engravings, rows of them, plates depicting pioneer scenes, black-and-white Americana. A colonial-looking painting of an old innkeeper with a clay pipe and a bright red nose, drinking from a pewter tankard, a brass plaque underneath the ornate gilt frame that said only "J.C. Waterson"—but was this the artist or the figure? He wouldn't have known many artists' names then, but he became an inhabitant of museums and galleries ever since, always his thing to do, days at a time, tirelessly, in whatever city he was visiting, always in one or another of them something sparking a memory from that night, what he had experienced in that house. That house seemed endless, room after room, hallways turning down hallways, each leading to a different, more spectacular space. It probably couldn't have been a David Hockney in the master bedroom, not back then, but he always remembered it as his—that sad, half-finished woman's figure in penciled lines. The kid no longer noticed or cared if he disturbed anyone by walking in a room, the naked couples tangled in sheets or humping away on cushions on the floors, not aware so much even if he were repeating a room. The visual angles entering a space differently made the pictures seem like new again, each repeated painting like a different painting, when once more taking it in, quietly, fixated on the walls, observing everything.

Nothing compared to what hung in the dining room. Entering there, all time stopped. It wasn't exactly a closed room—it had one wall standing alone as if to partition the area off from the rest of the big open living area, all under the same high arching roof beams that defined the space—he thought of it as the dining room because a polished cherrywood table and chairs with matching buffet were set up opposite that free-standing wall. Once he entered the area, the boy just stood there, rooted, gazing at this wall, amazed. Spilling into him was wonder enough to last a lifetime.

Imagine: for the first time, a kid of fifteen sees art, really *sees* it. Of course, he's sat through slide shows in school, not paying much attention, and sure, he's paged through a few books not really seeing. He's a drug addict, a sometimes prostitute, he recently committed his first violent crime. He's been facing these facts lately, and he feels rotten, wretched and rotten, like he's not worth the first breath he took when he was born, so he's never before been in such a stripped-down condition for receptivity. Imagine him that night walking through a house owned by a very rich family, wealthy enough to hang on its walls an incalculable fortune of the most valuable and noteworthy art. Around him, all through the house, a wild party is just reaching its most fevered state, half-naked people up and dancing to loud music in nearby rooms. The kid hears not one note of this, wouldn't notice one sweating nude body if it passed by, and more, he doesn't think a single thought now of who he is or what he's done or that he has no home. He suddenly knows, like a revelation, that everything will somehow work out, that good can and will happen in his life—he's sure now, as with an uplifting visitation.

The composition he was looking at took up the whole wall, about two times wider than he could stretch out both arms, and it reached from the floor almost to the ceiling. Space was filled with total faith in the expressive force of color, a use of full light without shadows, at its center a complete vision of life as a garden of simple flowers—sunny, serene, reassuring. It was all fluid, with curving lines, dazzling colors of leaves like flowers and of flowers like leaves, a vital impulse, animating nature, the picture swimming with other life in its bottom half as if life undersea, shapes like fishes, shells, coral, sponges, and, above the flowers, all in a row, faces, enigmatically cheerful faces, faces shaped like fruits, lines moving in elliptical swerves. The whole was as balanced as if made with a plumb line determining exactly straight verticals and forming with its opposite a perfect harmony on the horizontal, as though laid out with a compass, all cardinal directions represented, the dominating colors green, yellow, black, red, white, blue. Shapes radiated also in three dimensions, all made—he could see this up close—not from paint applied directly but with hundreds of pieces of paper cut out then painted on by the artist's now conceivable hands, glued there by the artist, what years later he would learn was a technique called *papiers découpés,* all composed from paper cut-outs. There was something about this, the idea of things applied to other things, which made him feel centered, somehow more himself. In the far background, up and to the left on the painted white space of the whole, black lines indicated in a most minimal way what must be a window, a synthesis of inside and outside, of the near and the far—he understood this to be saying something also about himself, the depth of it, and like a sure way out—mere suggestions of lines in pencil within the frame of the window creating the idea of looking out on what must be serene, settled weather in something very like a city, maybe not unlike the city nearby, a city he knew was out there, right now, in what would serve for him from that night on as something close to an eternal vision.

Of course, the boy knew nothing of any of this. He only knew what he could see in the most basic, most instinctive way, without putting anything into words. Still, he did sense his future, that he wouldn't be much longer living out on the streets—his luck would get better, something would save him, he was sure, without knowing how. Soon, he would be lifted out of this sordid life. His brother Harry would return from the war, disabled, yes—one hundred percent—disabled but still alive. His friend, Michael Fallon, not long afterwards, would be found at the bottom of a mineshaft in the mountains of Colorado, murdered—he would hear the story many years later—mistaken for a narc in a drug deal gone wrong. The boy didn't know any of this. Nothing of any of this mattered. His fear, the sense of doom he had felt himself falling into endlessly like into some bottomless concrete hole had fled away. All he knew now was that he was suddenly very happy.

The clock struck midnight. Shouts went up all over the house. *Happy New Year!* It was 1968. Everything in the world had changed. The celebration was lost on him. All he was able to do was keep gazing at the picture on the wall, transported by and committing to memory its vision, and trying to sound out the large painted signature in the bottom right corner, knowing nothing about French or even sure it was a French name. For some time after, he would mistakenly pronounce it in a way that rhymed with *lattice*, mouthing it over and over to himself—Hen-rey Mat-iss—like he had discovered the secret name of his personal god.

Looking for War

Yesterday, a woman asked me, what was it like?

Some people know a vague biography, that I've seen war. She asked me this question at one of those visiting writer's affairs, the obligatory dinner after the reading. We were at a Middle Eastern restaurant, the table spread abundantly with flat bread, hummus, stuffed grape leaves, falafels, tabbouleh and Israeli salads, the main course skewered lamb.

A television over the bar filled with eerie images from the newest war—quick edits of camera angles from jet cockpits, square targeting grids locking onto tanks, trucks, an airport runway, buildings, then the bombs were lasered in, each a streaking black pellet, followed by impassive spectacles like primitive video games, white flashes, roiling black-and-white explosions.

All of us at the table—intellectuals all—must have understood *the idea* that people were dying with each replay. But we didn't see them. We weren't meant to see them. We passed bread, served ourselves wine.

The woman sitting next to me asked again, *what was it like?* Not meaning to treat war casually, but still, wasn't there something else we could talk about at this meal?

She was pretty, a classic face with high cheekbones, perfect skin, and she projected a girlish adoration toward me, flirting in that way some girls have of reaching out a hand to touch my arm. This woman was a professional dancer as well as a poet, and she looked it—she carried herself with that athletic self-consciousness of her body in space. I have to admit that I was starting to fall for her a little until she asked that question. She wanted to know, needed to feel it, if only from someone who had seen. She tossed a neatly braided rope of red hair off her bare shoulder in an arrogantly flirtatious way. She leaned her dancer's body in closer and asked me again, someone not used to being denied, demanding this time, *so what was it like?*

What I didn't say—that my brother, Harry, lived with me now. He was a real veteran of war. War always would be with us in our house. She should by all rights be asking him not me. Harry had been living with me permanently since the separation from my wife, but on and off for years before that, since I had returned from a war in South America and got him out of the VA hospital, just signed him out, as simple as that, what they called an *AMA*—against medical advice.

I'll never forget the happy feeling that winter morning, settling into seats on the train, that special heightened consciousness, that elation, *we were still alive.* It didn't matter so much to me that Harry was giggling to himself like the gentle madman he had become, his face pressed against a window, a finger drawing shapes of numbers in the fog his breath made on the glass, then watching them disappear. We were two brothers braced against forward motion, me somehow expecting we could recapture our lives and live them differently. The air brakes of the train let loose, the car lurched ahead. The way our seats were facing, we were riding backwards into the city, and we've carried on like this, for years, looking behind us to the rest of our lives.

Year after year, in cycles, Harry started out living with me, at first in student apartments, later on in homes with my wife and daughter. We would make it OK together for a few months at least, until we got on each other's nerves. Then he would move out, try to make it on his own. We would set him up in apartments, in cheap rented rooms, on his disability checks. My wife or stepdaughter would get him a cat so he might not be so alone. Always, after a few months of this, he would end up off his medication. He had different explanations—he was tired of feeling so downed out all the time, or the medication made him impotent and *fuck it, man,* he'd say, *I just wanted to get laid.*

None of this told the real story. The sadness he carries is like hands reaching into his insides, squeezing, the grief of war never far away. It recedes for a while, can almost be forgotten, but it always returns, suddenly, like a seasonal flood. He turned his cats loose into the neighborhood. And I would find him weeks later, homeless, out on the streets not so differently than the way we had lived sometimes when we were kids. Or a call came in from a social worker in some hospital psych ward in a distant city explaining that he had been brought in by the police, was being held for observation, *a danger to himself and others.* I would travel to wherever it was, sign him out. He would move back in with me again. This has been our cycle, years and years. We're brothers. We've always been each other's keepers.

He was doing much better recently, as if leveling out, staying on his meds, his anti-psychotic pills, keeping to a daily routine like a religion. Mostly, he watches TV, old movies in black-and-white, endless reruns on cable, "Hawaii Five-O," "The Rockford Files," "The Dick Van Dyke Show," "Cheers," never tiring of seeing the same movies and episodes over again as if comforted by their repetition, lying half-sleeping on his couch. He does keep up with the news, which we watch together most evenings. In between, he walks two times a day to the stores, cooks his meals, vacuums the carpets, feeds the dog, keeps the lawn green. Sometimes, he picks up a harmonica and tinkers around.

Nights, he retires to his room and scribbles in notebooks. He has two tall bookcases full of these spiral notebooks stacked one on top of the other. There must be at least five hundred of them, each an inch thick. Most of what he writes is scattered thinking, schizophrenic diaries, *outlet for his psychosis*, as the psychiatrist he pays for privately—he wants as little as possible to do with VA doctors now—calls them, incomprehensible scribbling but filled with phrases that jump up off the page with clear rationality when they can be deciphered from his enraged handwriting. He doesn't want me to read them. Examples from today, noted quickly by sneaking into his room: *what they did to me...these people...they won't leave me alone... this is all because of them...the voices are real...real is what they send me to see...there must be more to civilization than mammals, insects will take over the earth...the ones who really killed Kennedy...these blue dots...we'll have them killed...we'll kill them all no mercy...bomb the shit out of them...kill them...*

And so on. My brother is reacting badly to the new war on TV. Even as he's trying to live in his own way a more or less regular life, he's suddenly drenched like by a thunderstorm. He's started leaping off his couch in jerky, compulsive energy bursts, throwing himself to the floor and doing pushups on the carpet—fingertip pushups—a thousand a day, I've counted, in sets of fifty. In between sets of pushups, he slams out the side door of our house, jogs down the block and around the park at least four times a day, which must add up to ten miles. We both know what he's doing. He's preparing himself, getting ready just in case. On the other hand, I've taken up cigarettes again after being so proud of myself for quitting. We haven't talked about this. He does his pushups. I walk around the house lighting one after the other as if I'd rather commit slow suicide than have to think about any war again. We keep putting on a face, pretending we're perfectly dry. We don't talk about it. We don't need to say anything.

Recently, I came downstairs in the middle of the night for another pack of cigarettes. I had been fighting with my girlfriend, one of those stupid arguments born of too much stress and tension that can rise from out of nowhere, mostly my fault for being so on edge. We had said ugly things no one should ever say. Our voices must have been loud enough to wake the neighbors. We were able to recover only by just stopping. *Stop!*, she shouted. She was right. We held each other, saying we were sorry. But I was upset, smoked out, came downstairs. I found my brother in his underwear, sitting on his couch, his TV dark. He wasn't usually up this late. The way he looked at me gave me an instant jolt of panic that he had quit taking his pills. He was an old man suddenly, gray hair hanging at his shoulders, his gaunt, starved expression hollowed out with exhausted sadness, his old soldier's defeat. He said flatly, without bitterness, as if sharing a mere fact, "Not once in my life has a woman said she loves me."

Yesterday, the pretty woman at the table flipped her rope of long hair, demanding, *so what was it like?*

"It's hard to remember," I answered, finally. "Whatever happened, it was over like *that*," I said, snapping my fingers right in her face to make her jump.

There was a time in my life when I went looking for war. Part of this was for classic reasons common to many men—as a way to prove myself, establish my fame. If I were to die in war then so be it; if I were to stay alive, it would be on certain terms, as in the funeral speech of Pericles: *Choosing to die resisting, rather than to live submitting, they fled only from dishonor, met danger face to face, and after one brief moment, while at the summit of their fortune, escaped, not from their fear but from their glory.*

I had never seen a war except on TV—video reports from correspondents doing stand-ups in safari jackets set against chaotic green backgrounds, sounds of distant gunfire, B-52s dropping bombs from their bellies like great shitting birds, orange explosions, black smoke, drumbeating helicopter blades, newscaster voices narrating shaky footage of soldiers hunkering low or slogging through rice paddies or humping sandbags, muddy roads teeming with the fleeing dispossessed, shell-shocked peasant faces in close-ups, pure human misery bleeding through the screen.

Watching, I knew I was missing something. I couldn't even sit and watch but had to leap up and pace around the room, frustrated and enraged. *Damnit*, I should be *there* instead of where I was. Not that I hadn't been in battles—peace marches and sit-ins, with nightsticks, teargas, handcuffs, police vans. As a journalist for the free presses, I had been there for all of this, the grief-stricken shouting after students were shot down by government soldiers at Kent State, the roiling tens of

thousands marching on Washington, chanting, cat-calling, those
days of rage.

More than this, I had lived through a military regime in
Argentina when I had been an exchange student, was even
shot at in a car while racing away with student *compañeros*
from painting walls with the deliriously oxymoronic symbol
and slogan:

P

J V P *¡Muerte a la dictadura!*

Which signified: *Perón returns. Peronist Youth.* Ironically
juxtaposed to: *Death to the dictatorship!*

We believed with deluded madness in our imaginary desire,
that the return of strongman Juan Perón from exile to power
could mean a promised social democracy.

I had been arrested three times in Argentina at street demonstrations, the third time had my head split open like a
grapefruit. My adopted family bribed my way, still bleeding,
out of the detention center. And I finally followed their advice,
with some good luck, in applying to college back in the USA.
I said quick *hasta pronto* to my militant buddies to take up an
offer for loans and cafeteria jobs to work my way through
the vaunted University of Chicago, notorious at that time for
accepting neurotic, politically minded students, even one with
an unorthodox, patched together school record like my own
that showed big unexplainable gaps between eighth grade in
the U.S. and a diploma in Buenos Aires, half a world away,
awarded by an obscure private academy run by militant French
priests. I returned to the United States with leftist dreams,
idealistic visions of revolution, *all power to the people.* After
two years at Chicago, I had compiled a police file for civil

disruption two inches thick, along with a clippings portfolio from the free presses about half that thickness filled with articles carrying my byline or written under a pseudonym. This was the Nixon era of harassment of the press and quasi-fascist *dirty tricks*. Some of my journalist colleagues claimed to have had their phones tapped, their mail stolen, their apartments broken into, their research and notes mysteriously vanishing. Many of us agreed to use the same pseudonym as a protest, "Frank Malebranch," for our most anti-government stories. Under my own name, I had placed several freelance photos with UPI, United Press International, that now ruined, once major wire service. My best photos were of antiwar demonstrations, battles in the streets. A few had been published in newspapers all over the globe.

So I thought I was going places in journalism, my college grades were high, but this wasn't enough. My slow conclusion was that I had to *fight back from the inside*, make the ultimate sacrifice, get my head shaved. I became obsessed with the idea of enlisting, fantasized about secretly slipping my fellow grunts in basic copies of *The Daily Worker* and preaching to buck privates the Marxist ideology direct from the streets of The Movement that *all private property is theft*, explaining that, though I was a committed Socialist against the war, I could no longer buy into the bourgeois elitism of college deferments while the working class and repressed minorities did most of the fighting and dying. From the bunkers, I would write articles for the free presses that *subverted the system from within*. Then suddenly, that war was all but over. The United States had lost. What would sacrificing myself for *that* ever prove?

And there was my brother, Harry. He had been sent over there, drafted in a sense but not really, since a judge gave him the choice to volunteer or go directly to prison after a bust for marijuana possession, so he enlisted. He came back from Vietnam after seven months of his combat tour to spend the next two years in hospitals—first good Army facilities, in Japan, in Denver, then he was discharged and dumped off like a sack of trash into the callow neglect of the VA institutions. They shipped him out straight into the Psycho Corps—our troops in gray pajamas, tens of thousands of them like a jittering, babbling voodoo army wandering hallways and grounds, rubber slippers and filthy smocks like uniforms, this new branch of the disarmed services composed of post-Vietnam crazies, it was dawning on me, Harry might be serving in to the end of his days.

We sat together on splintery benches on the campus of the crumbling VA hospital in Northport, Long Island. I would take the train out there then walk. It was two miles from the railroad station through the quaint town like something out of a Norman Rockwell painting then up a hill on a road lined with sugar maple trees to that collection of run-down, red brick buildings with roofs of busted shingles, ragged grounds messy with rotting leaves. I would sign in at the desk of my brother's ward. All the nurses came from somewhere else, Asian countries, mostly, the Philippines or Korea or Indonesia. They spoke mainly broken English. A lot of the inmates suffered from the delusion they had been captured by gooks and were prisoners of war. I never spoke to Harry's doctor—not even sure he had a doctor—but the ward nurse always said his condition was unchanged. His diagnosis: *schizophrenic reaction to wartime stress.*

I would get a pass to take Harry out for some air. We weren't supposed to leave the grounds. He would be waiting for me in the day room, slumping in a battered folding chair in front of a TV where the picture was always snowy or rolling. Nobody cared. My brother was a starved-looking version of his former self, broomstick arms hanging out his gray tie-back hospital smock with trails of food and juice stains down the front. His feet barely shuffled along, his Thorazine stagger. Drug side-effects kept his hands cramped up, fingers curled like blunted talons. They had left his fingernails to grow out, long and filthy. His hair was unwashed, uncombed, sticking out every which way in a wild growth. His blue rubber slippers were peppered with cigarette burns. No amount of my complaint forms or angry confrontations with VA staff made any difference to change this negligent treatment, this lack of any care. This was America, after all. This was a wounded warrior's reward. We sat together mostly in silence under the unkempt trees. We passed a joint. In those days, staffers at the VAs quietly recommended marijuana for the post-traumatic effects of war. It kept the patients more subdued. The inmates from Vietnam stayed as stoned as possible most of the time, not that an uninformed observer would have noticed much difference.

What Harry had been through, I mostly didn't know. He had served as a door gunner on a helicopter in the Asha Valley. He had *volunteered* for combat duty, something that made me envious, disgusted and proud all at once. There had been a severe shortage of door gunners during that brutal campaign. All I had managed to put together about his combat experience was that, because of this door gunner shortage, they had given my brother too many doses of amphetamines during the battle to keep him going, a *sustained action*, it was called. He didn't sleep for two weeks. He burned his hands raw changing out red-hot M-60 barrels. In combat, he just forgot. He showed me the scars, like the lines on his palms had melted into shiny white smears. They had sent him up again with hands wrapped in gauze. One evening, he got back to base around dinner time, jumped out of his Huey, marched straight into the officer's mess tent. He popped off two smoke grenades, one yellow and one red, bowling them out between the tables. He could laugh at his memory of all those officers hitting the deck, diving under tables, coughing and choking, crawling in panic for air. Everything else was a mystery, what exactly he had seen, what he had experienced of war, and if he had actually killed another human being.

War was something he almost never spoke about. Whenever I prodded him, he would tell bits and pieces of his story of panicked officers taking cover in red and yellow smoke. He laughed, more a crazed high giggling than real laughter. This had nothing to do with the pot. Pot smoked under such circumstances had no effect to get us high, it was just harsh, deadening smoke. I told him I was thinking about enlisting. His laugh shut off like with a switch. His starved face went slack, jaw dropping open, a line of drug-induced drool trailed from his lower lip. But his green eyes were sharp, jumped to either side as if he were seeing dark outer things or invisible people—he had said more than once what he saw were *blue dots*. Without turning to me, as if speaking for the sake of whatever he was wary of in the air, he said, "Don't go. Don't even think about it. Not over there."

He retreated back into his usual silence. I don't know why that bothered me so much, how he wouldn't say more, except that I was obsessed to know, needed the experience even if only through him of what it was like—the fear, the danger, smells of gunpowder and cordite, the hot pressure of an exploding mortar round like a hurricane-force desert wind. I *had* to be there. I *had* to know what it was.

One cold autumn afternoon we sat like this, worse than this because we said so little to each other that I was beginning to wonder why I was making the effort to hump it out here at least once a month, hitchhiking maybe twenty hours from Chicago to Manhattan then catching an expensive train to see him, like what difference did it make, anyway? They had turned him into a zombie. Or maybe he was holding out on me intentionally, after all we had been through together. We had spent three years, on and off, taking care of each other as homeless kids, had slept in hippie crash pads, cheap hotels, even in a cardboard box, had rebounded *home*, such as it was, then suffered and run away again, in cycles, from the torment and physical abuse of our parents. There was a time when we had *kept each other alive*. And it was like a violation of brother-hood to think he was holding out on me now, consumed by my self-pitying feelings of loneliness and betrayal, that sense of broken trust hitting like quick cold stomach cramps so I actually sat leaning over, arms wrapped around my middle. Or I would have to stand up off the bench and pace around in aimless circles, kicking at the wet rotting leaves, holding back shouts of rage.

I decided then and there I would go find my own war. There were plenty of wars out there, *damnit*, I was going to find one. No matter that I was only a year away from a college degree— one of those Great Books general studies programs heavy with literature, foreign languages, the Greeks—doing more than OK by any outward standards, especially considering what we had come from. Still, my life felt pointless, filled with days one knows are forgettable, books and lectures blurring into meaningless phrases, empty words one would never recall. I just couldn't *let it all pass me by*.

On my return to Chicago, I readied myself, working out in the gym, running laps, processing paperwork for a leave of absence for next quarter while at the same time defrauding banks by taking out new college loans. I was going off to war. It would have to be a war no one knew much about. That way, I could write free press stories and take photographs. Maybe I could pull off a good enough article to sell to a major magazine. Why not? In the right kind of war, hell, I might even make my reputation.

So it came to pass that I found myself trudging through undergrowth in a dense *artificial* forest, on my way to a war—artificial because we were moving through some kind of immense Argentine tree farm recently purchased by the multinational wood products subsidiary of Shell Oil Renewables South America, that oil company as ubiquitous as any ancient god. The trees had been planted there two decades ago, a test forest seeking to discover some balance of commercial and native species that might also sustain wildlife. The test forest had been declared a failure, sold out to Shell, scheduled for clear-cutting and replacement planting with a monoculture consisting of genetically manipulated pines.

My guide, a Guaraní Indian *compañero* in the militancy named Sikín, was explaining this to me in melodious, breathy commentary as I followed his sweated-through, coarse peasant shirt back through showering twigs, leaves, bits of branches flying up from his whacking machete blade, steel scraping and ringing with each rhythmic stroke, clearing bamboo-like undergrowth from an old log skidder trail in a jungle he spoke of with apologetic sadness, as though he blamed himself, as if it were his own failed garden. He slashed along ahead of me, lamenting the scarcity of white *quebrachos* and incense trees, and the near disappearance of the *palo trébol* tree with its medicinal bark—he used the Spanish name for the endangered tree, so valued for its hard golden wood and indigenous medicine,

Amburana cearensis, known as the *cumaseba* in Peru and *jacaranda do brejo* in Brazil, not to be confused with the same Spanish word, *trébol*, common name for ground-crawling clover abundant almost everywhere. By the end of the 20th century—nearly thirty years after Sikín and I labored that day through his beloved jungle—due to wholesale logging and slash-and-burn agriculture, the *palo trébol* had so diminished in numbers that the United Nations estimated no more than two hundred old growth examples were left standing in the lower Paraná region, so few that, a generation later, many people had forgotten this tree ever existed.

Rolling off Sikín's tongue and up through his nose in sing-song tones were Guaraní names for other trees—*kurupa'yra, tagyhu, peterevy, yvyaraneti, urunde'ymi*—trees which used to grow abundantly in the region, meaningless to me except for the musical sound of their names. Animal species were vanishing, the *oso hormiguero grande*—the anteater bear—the gray fox, two kinds of exotic peccaries, and the *tatú carreta*, which I understood to be a kind of armadillo as big as a wheelbarrow. The beloved jungle of his childhood used to be filled with colorful birds, rare green parrots, gorgeous blue and gold macaws. Patrolling helicopters of the armed forces of Paraguay and Argentina—Bell Helicopter Hueys, part of *anti-Communist aid* from the United States—the thumping noise and turbulent winds of their blades beating low just over the treetops caused parrots and macaws to drop dead out of their nests from fright. The ones that didn't drop dead abandoned their nests and flew off, never to be seen again. The forest we were slashing through seemed empty of birds. Sikín was a walking encyclopedia of jungle fauna and flora on the way to extinction. I was getting the idea that his war wasn't as much with enemy troops across the border, on the other side of the rivers, as with *the forces of economic development* despoiling the whole immense Paraná and Amazonian riparian zones, seeking to turn his patria Guaraní—his tribal Fatherland, as he called it with a nostalgia that already predicted its defeat—into one incalculably huge and profitable agribusiness plantation.

What I didn't tell him was that I believed, as Borges, that *nadie es la patria*—no one is a *patria*. By extension nor could be any tribe of men. But I disagreed with Borges that men should nevertheless aspire to be worthy of such patriotic oaths. How could anyone claim to be fighting for a Socialist vision of *the International* and still speak that hateful word, no less than a proverbial curse on all mankind, *patria*? *Fatherland*, with its flag-waving, fascist connotations. I didn't say anything. Sikín was the contact given to me through friends of friends, as is the way of so much journalism, to guide me to a revolution.

The revolution now had a human face, fine featured like most Guaraní, disarmingly not very traditionally American Indian looking but more similar, say, to faces of southern Italian peoples, without the Roman nose, his skin a coffee-with-cream brown. He had a tall muscular body he carried erect with held-in dignity, as if powered by his awareness of centuries of struggle by his people, his persistent resignation to *carry on the fight*, as he kept saying, like he had been born with it as a duty, *the fight for my people*.

Listening to Sikín, I could be filled with the power of his belief, that this was *a war for liberation*. The way he spoke such inspiring platitudes, one burn-scarred white lid naked of eyelashes lowering halfway over a wandering milky eye—an injury from his youth, trying to make a pipe bomb that exploded in his face—he took on a harsh but seductive look, especially when he had a few drinks in him. That eye suddenly fastened on something, on some enemy he could see in memory or in the air, the scarred lid lowering over it, giving him the hard, cold look of an experienced killer, a warrior's capacity to size up any man as if already drawing a machete with murderous intimacy across his throat. I had seen this look before, in street thieves, in gang kids who carried guns in New York, mostly when they were paranoid and crazy on meth highs. There were a lot of men with that look along this riverfront, in bars filled with scarred, ragged characters, smugglers, the *mensú*, the contract laborers at the edge of homicidal drunks, fresh from logging camps or plantations up the rivers. The Paraná region where three countries meet is legendary for its frontier roughness.

The only name I knew him by was that one name, Sikín. He had a Spanish name, Juan or José María or Fernando, but he refused to use it, insisting on his name in Guaraní. Like most children of *indio* exiles, Sikín had learned from his parents the sing-song language of Guaraní, their patriotic vision of Paraguay as expressed in a lyric tradition called *ocara potÿ*—wild flower—the sentimental nationalism in songs and mythic incantations that many of the leaders of the resistance movements could recite from memory and which, from what I could comprehend, envisioned Paraguay, despite its bloody history, as some perpetual Eden blessed with an abundance of innocence and bananas.

The day before, we rode hour after hour in his pickup, out through the scrubby brown grass plains of the Chaco, where the cows looked like racks of bones covered by sun-burnt hides. We bucked our way off on a system of rutted dirt roads through mud hut and tin-roofed cinderblock villages filled with scattering chickens and barefoot, big-eyed *indio* children who chased after us with shouts of glee, dark mothers staring out darker doorways, then we were off again on the rough roads.

Here and there, as we passed, small flocks of Ñandues—Rhea ostriches—would leap up out of tall grass, fleeing in gangly comic dances on stick-like legs into groves of thorny trees.

I wasn't paying much attention to landscape. From time to time, I lifted my camera and took a few miserly shots, conserving film. I was thinking about what lay ahead, that if I could just pass their tests, get on the good side of the *guerrilleros*, they might take me with them deep into the jungles to see, close up, exactly what I was looking for.

Not that there wasn't some good talk to pass the hours, and going over with Sikín my rudimentary Guaraní, a language whose high nasal vowels and frequent throaty trilling sounds I could barely get my mouth around. Guaraní is similar to Polynesian languages in the way it strings together, and in a way to Japanese—tone alters words. There are nasal vowels, like high humming notes through a tenor kazoo, and trillings in the back of the throat, like whispered garglings. Intoned either way, these sounds transform one word into another. I kept referring to a book I carried in my bag—it was later destroyed—the hardcover edition of *El Idioma Guaraní: gramática y antología de prosa y verso*, by a Jesuit priest whose name I can't recall. In the bucking pickup truck, I flipped to a list of phrases in Guaraní with Spanish translations which were comprehensible only by knowing certain juxtapositions. The specific often acts as the generic in Guaraní, one idea stands for similar ideas. Saying a thing often also signifies something else as well as itself—money is *pira pire*, literally, fish skin, like the silvery shine of coins; an airplane is *curuzu veve*, the cross that flies; *the wing of the bird* stands for *half of the distance* to somewhere; *the justice of God* is a phrase widely used for *medicinal fruits*, and so on—which I understood to be like Shakespeare or Homer using *a thousand sail* for *a thousand ships,* only it was far more complex than that, more deeply encoded than any European language ever imagined being. I had been listening to Guaraní for days in the riverfront bars, and when Sikín spoke it with contacts. It seemed to me not so much a spoken language as a kind of singing filled with high reverberating hums and low airy tones, a music like indigenous wooden flutes. Guaraní phrases kept slipping and sliding over each other fluidly, like mixing river currents, in an endless substitution, an infinitely recycling metonymy. As we rode along, Sikín listened patiently to me butchering phrases from the book. "It's really easy to learn Guaraní," he teased. "All you have to do is be born here, speak it about thirty years, and you know it perfectly."

Guaraní is more complicated than its difficulty with nasals, trillings and juxtapositions. Though most verbs are made up of two syllables, they can be almost infinitely agglutinated to make contextually precise conjugations. The verb *to clean*—I was taught this when we stopped for a supper of rice and boiled beef in a spicy sauce, served on a plank table, in lantern-light, by a lonely country store owner's wife, who kept giving Sikín flirtatious sneers like a challenge, demanding a response as she cleared our plates—could be made into a nine syllable conjugation, a single word intoned through the nose, meaning, *did you clean it all up yet?* It was dizzying: a localized vocabulary yet a myriad of precise ways to add syllables for specific situations. Sikín's good eye was directed at the wife as she bent over a red plastic tub, giving her hip a little haughty kick each time she wiped a plate pulled out of the soapy water. She was plump as a guayaba fruit, especially in her hips, shaped like a pear, but she had a pretty face, puffing her cheeks like a blowfish then letting short haughty laughs out between her fleshy lips. Blue flies buzzed our plates. She stood over us, waving them off, her pure heat a warm homey perfume like rising bread. She was alone, as were so many Guaraní women, her husband off for months on contract labor, or across the river to the war. Sikín got us all going on the verb *to love*, like a game—*jahohayhu*, the verb in Guaraní for *love between human beings*, though stating this like an infinitive, out of context, might be a little confusing to a native speaker, who would understand *we love each other*, since there are no infinitives, no such detachment is possible, verbs only make sense depending on the specific situations in which they are used.

Sikín hoisted the woman's runny-nosed children up onto his lap, showing them off as if they were his own. As best I could comprehend, he added syllables and complements to the root *hayhu* in a phrase which conveyed love for a daughter before she reaches puberty, another for when she becomes a woman, then another for when she marries. He set the little girl down and lifted up the little boy, making the phrase expressing the love of a father for his young son, another for when the son reaches manhood. The kid looked at me with owl eyes, holding out his shredded chewed stub of raw sugar cane, inviting me to share.

For a man and a woman, he jokingly showed off subtle variations expressing love for both before and after making love. Sikín repeated these verb phrases heavy with implications, directed at the store owner's wife, and I thought I could see her fleshy legs turn red from her skirt down to the walked-over heels of her rope soled shoes. In Sikín's language, it was as if *now* is what really matters, *when* something happens indicated by framing particles and words if needed—as in *yesterday-we-love-each-other, last-week-we-love-each-other, a-year-ago-we-love-each-other*, and *we-love-each-other-in-the-future*. Sikín went down the list, making me repeat after him, as the woman served us glasses of *caña*—cane liquor. What I thought I was sure of out of this game was that, as it might have been said in his Guaraní, *Sikín-and-the-woman-love-each-other-tonight*. But he made it clear after our drink, no, we had another hour of driving before sleeping. He left money on the table. Calling her *compañera*, accepting her regretful clinging embraces, her wet kisses on our cheeks, we said goodnight. We escaped into the darkness.

We spent the night in an empty Shell company storage shed at the edge of the tree farm. Sikín hung two hammocks that smelled of motor oil by low hooks in the mud walls of the hut. We swung into them, our bodies just barely clearing the dirt floor. Sikín took off his boots, rolled to his side. He instantly fell asleep with an easy breathing. I lay awake. This was the first time I had ever tried sleeping in a hammock, and, closing my eyes, it was a strange feeling, like being hung out over some immense space. With every swing, my body started up as if trying to catch itself from falling. Cockroaches the size of sparrows buzzed through the air. A spider as big as the spread fingers of my hand hung in a web in one corner of the tin roof, darkly visible in a crack of moonlight. None of this bothered me. I was all impatience and anticipation for what might happen in the morning. And, after all, I had spent nights in far worse places. I found the bottle of scotch in my bag, drank some, then finally fell asleep.

Before dawn, Sikín was ready by the truck, sipping *mate* tea through a nickel straw from a gourd. I joined him, the warm bitter tea soothing, as stimulating as coffee.

We readied our bags. I checked to make sure my camera was on top, loaded, lenses within easy reach. Sikín opened the glove compartment of the truck and I saw him slip a big black pistol with extra clips into his bag. I hadn't known it was there. I swallowed, dry in the mouth, reminded where we were going, what I was looking for.

Sikín said we should get moving before the sun got too hot, we would be on foot now until we reached the river. I tried to joke with him, saying how it wouldn't be as hot as what he'd missed last night. Last night, he seemed to enjoy my allusions to what could have happened. Not this morning. "Too many men end up face down in the river," he said. "In any case, I'm married."

This surprised me, his first reference that he had a wife. I had assumed he had no family. I'd have asked more, but something in the way that milky eye fixed on me made it clear he regretted letting me know even this much about his family, as if letting people know too much could get them killed.

We started off through the jungle, that failed tree farm, that artificial forest. He pulled out his machete. He started slashing the way ahead of us, through bamboo-like undergrowth. We set off down the old log skidder trail. He began to list the musical *indio* names of trees, telling me about his jungle as if he were ashamed, as if it were his own failed garden. He lamented the loss of the animals, the birds, the scarcity of certain trees, white *quebrachos* and incense trees, especially the *palo trébol* tree, gone nearly extinct. He turned to me with a bitter laugh. He began singing a string of syllables in a verb phrase in his Guayakí-Guaraní dialect. All I could make out were the root sounds of the verb for love. As best as I could comprehend, it signified, *I love you, my middle-aged wife, medicine gathering at the palo trébol tree.*

Sikín repeated this long gurgling brook of a verb phrase several times as we worked our way through the bush. Slowly, his point sank in. For his people, the extinction of a tree meant wiping out forever one way to express love.

Not that I paid so much attention to this at the time. I didn't say that I didn't care much for Sikín's jungle, its trees, its animals. Everything in it seemed poisonous, a hassle, full of thorns. Just being out in nature like this caused in me a terrible and irresistible compulsion to start chain-smoking. My head felt like it was packed with hot dirty wash cloths. My stomach fluttered with bouts of nausea from anti-malaria pills. It was tough to breathe in the wet tropical atmosphere, less oxygen than superheated steam. It was hard to see with sweat dripping into my eyes in the green half-darkness of the overhanging trees. In about ten minutes, I was hardly able to focus on anything more than taking just one more step, one more breath, one more step. And so we moved on through the jungle.

My right boot slipped in something gooey. A sickening stench billowed up like a sweet spray of rotten fish. A little involuntary shout of disgust escaped me. I stopped, kicking, trying to shake a clinging, dripping glob of stuff off my boot.

Sikín turned, pushed back his straw hat. *Ay-ha!*—he let loose this strange sound, half laughter, half an expression of surprise. His wandering milky eye rolled independently of the other with a wary glance at my boot. In his slow, lilting *indio* Spanish, he said, "Old nest of *zacaruyú* snakes."

I froze. I understood I'd stepped into a small sinkhole of eggs with numerous decayed, half-born hatchlings. I didn't have the chance or breath to ask follow-ups like *what kind of snakes? Were the snakes venomous?* Sikín gestured with his machete and said, "Many snakes in the trees," then he signaled urgently we should press on ahead. That was right on with me. We started to do this, with me looking only at my boots, ready for snakes.

Something hard cracked me dead center on the forehead.

Owww—my eyes shut in a reactive squint. More things

began raining down, rock-like, green, spiny hard fruits like horse chestnuts, a bombardment of them pelting us from all directions. We both ducked instinctively and covered our heads. Sikín's good eye looked up with a surprised fear and I was also afraid. Leaves jumped around in chaos. The red jungle earth was hopping with these rock-like things—like green apricots with tough ridges—but most of them bouncing around only *after* they hit our bodies. They felt like a flurry of small left hooks punching into my back and ribs.

We heard them then, barking, *ooking,* one or two deep-throated, male-dominant screams. I pulled a forearm from in front of my eyes and saw quick movements, black-brown leaping creatures the size of cats high in the trees. Far up, in twos and threes, they swung down, hanging by their prehensile tails, fuzzy brown arms winging the green missiles with perfect aim, *whizzz-bap!* Right on the nose if I hadn't lifted my arms to block them. *Monkeys?*

The few breaks of sky between high branches were black with their movements, diving and swooping like some horrifying flock of huge wingless bats. Common Tufted or Brown Capuchin monkeys—the kind often domesticated and turned into cute little organ-grinder monkeys in crackerjack hats begging for tips—*Cebus apella* have rarely been known to gather in troops of more than ten to fifteen. But I swear there were hundreds of them up there that day, everywhere flying around in fantastic acrobatic shows from branch to branch through the trees. They were nasty, white fangs flashing, like rabid dogs, barking, snarling, crying out in gleeful screams, *giving it everything they had* in an outraged, coordinated attack to drive two puny human invaders off their turf.

All of a sudden, this incredible number of green rock seeds came at us, like a big backpack full of them fired shotgun style, whipping into us like from a hundred slingshots all at once. Three hit dead center on my skull, no use what I did fighting them off. A half-conscious thought struck home that they could stone us to death—*stoned to death by monkeys?*—if we didn't start running.

We started running. We crashed through the undergrowth, bamboo stuff tearing at us. We bulled our way through, me falling behind Sikín, my shoulder bag catching on branches so I had to stop and rip it free. We flung our bodies headlong like two mad bears through the snapping and slashing brush crying out, *¡Ay! ¡Vámonos! ¡Corramos! Run!*

Green rockets pursued us, cracking and walloping at our backs. So it went until we finally saw light up ahead. We broke through, spilling out of the trees into tall marsh grass and knee-deep muck of the riverbank. We plunged, waded, fell on our faces, fought our way to a raised area of harder mud bank where we didn't sink in so much, where we could throw ourselves sprawling to the ground, out of breath. We looked like we had just been keel-hauled along the river bottom, soaked through, mud and leaves clinging everywhere, rips in our clothes, faces scratched and bleeding.

Sikín sheathed his machete. He looked at his watch with his good eye, his milky eye roving around at the dark forest and as if to include me in its hypervigilance. We were behind schedule. And he had lost his hat. Still, we needed to rest. Heatstroke was always a danger here. He found shade under some brush and we both moved in under it to catch our breath. Heat pressed around us, squeezing like smothering arms.

Ahead of us flowed the Río Pilcomayo—it was at the end of the rainy season, the river and marshlands in receding flood— like an inland sea of reddish, sleepily moving water. A low scrub jungle formed a hazy green line far off on the other bank—scruffy thorn trees natural to this part of the world looking like a jagged green comb missing teeth, wavering in a mirage of intense heat. Behind us, the darker green dense wall of the tree farm went eerily silent, as if nothing had ever stirred in there. Nothing moved, not even a bird calling in the distance, like nothing had happened.

Across the river was Paraguay. It was a mysterious country to me even after reading everything I could get my hands on about it—naively nationalistic works like *El alma de la raza* by Manuel Domínguez, more objective accounts such as Warren's *Paraguay, An Informal History*, along with numerous sobering reports by Amnesty International and the United Nations Commission on Human Rights. I had read about Paraguay's tragic history of shrinking borders from the grand nation it had once been when it took up the whole center of South America. It had been the seat of the Jesuit empire of the seventeenth and eighteenth centuries, which had converted the Guaraní to Christianity and sought to organize native peoples into rational communities based on classical Greek ideas of the *free polis*—self-determining, ideal towns of five thousand citizens each, with communal farms and fields, community centers which included something like cafeterias and even day care centers, each with a large paved plaza fronted by a church. About a hundred of these towns had been carved out of the jungles of Latin America, in an orderly chessboard plan, at measured distances from one another, at least thirty-one of them in Paraguay. As many as 150,000 Guaraní lived in them at one time, many of these tiny cities still being discovered, red stone ruins still being cleared of the jungle undergrowth and oblivion of centuries. The Jesuit-Guaraní empire fell because of a war with Spain and Portugal, in league with the Papacy, to establish the slave trade, *latifundio* land grants, and harsh conquistador rule by imperial charters from European kings. Guaraní not killed or captured and enslaved simply vanished from these Jesuit towns, and along with them, half a million who had resisted living in the towns fled further back into the jungles.

In the early nineteenth century, Paraguay was caught up in wars of independence from Spain that overwhelmed the whole continent. Internecine feuding followed, led by egomaniacal generals and self-serving politicians, that snake stew of South American history that killed any democratic dreams of continental unity. Of the liberators, José de San Martín died in lonely exile in France, spurned, and believing he had been forgotten. Simón Bolívar bitterly proclaimed his own epitaph, *I've plowed the sea*. In Paraguay, a repressive strong man's government eventually rose up from the stew, headed by a first-rate schemer, a lawyer turned self-styled, tinpot emperor named José Gaspar Rodríguez de Francia, *beloved of his people, father of his country*. He called himself *El Supremo*, and, despite Paraguayan historical myth, *beloved of his people, father of his country*, his nation subsisted in misery for thirty years. A brief progressive era something like a Republic followed his death, but politicians sold land to foreign companies, who ended up owning fifty percent of Paraguay's resources, the other half controlled by an oligarchy of fewer than one hundred families.

Then there was war with Brazil, Argentina and Uruguay, from 1864–1870, in which much of Paraguay's territory was seized, more than ninety percent of its male population killed off in a cataclysmic and seldom written about thievery and devastation. Perhaps 500,000 men died, more dead than could be reliably counted by those who survived. One sad statistic is that the ratio of women to men left in the capital city of Asunción was something like 28 to 1, and women outnumbered men 10 to 1 in the remoter countryside. A succession of autocratic leaders ruled after this war, acting more or less as paid-off trade representatives for Brazil and Argentina. Brief but bloody civil wars broke out from time to time, feuding members of the ruling oligarchy recruiting repressed *indios* into ragtag troops in the name of *democratic reforms* or *to overthrow repression.*

Another war was declared in the 1930s against Bolivia, for *national honor*, over an insignificant wedge of northern plains in the Chaco region erroneously thought to be rich with petroleum. Both countries lost an estimated 100,000 dead and effectively bankrupted themselves fighting over what, in the end, amounted to a big empty cattle ranch. So Paraguay had degenerated into what it was now, a seldom-mentioned backwater of the known world, barely making it on a few scruffy wheat and soy bean fields, low grade tobacco, orange groves, scrawny cattle, banana and *yerba mate* tea plantations, by logging its jungles into wastelands and, after World War II, by taking protection money from ex-Nazis and anyone else who would pay the price for safe haven from war crimes.

Paraguay had been ruled since 1954 by a ruthless dictator, General Alfredo Stroessner, a living exemplar and admirer of Adolf Hitler. This dictator sought to preserve the European descended, land-holding oligarchy and foreign business concerns in power—the one percent who owned ninety percent of the land. And he made further land deals carved out of wilderness and Indian tribal homelands favorable to this officially Spanish-speaking—many were now also German-speaking—ruling class. He transformed Paraguay into a smuggler's paradise, with planeloads of liquor, cigarettes, blue jeans, electronics, consumer goods of all kinds, later, illegal drugs, flown in every day to be sold across the rivers to black markets in Argentina, Bolivia and Brazil.

Coming back across the rivers were stolen goods. Paraguay became like a huge fencing operation for various mafias of thieves from all over South America. Stroessner's regime put in place an infamous "24-hour auto registration law" that permitted any stolen car that turned up in Paraguay to be given a "clear" title after one day, for a fee—called *mau* cars— then they could be "legally" sold.

Along with all of this, President-for-life Stroessner had been carrying out what amounted to a sinister program of enforced peonage and genocide on the jungle Indians—the Guayakí, Ayoreo, Mbyá, Aché, Avá Chiripá, Paí Tavyterá and other tribes, most of them Guaraní-speaking, having been wiped out by as many as 100,000 killed during the years of his rule. The *indios* of Paraguay had been subjected to organized hunts to kill them, some actually chartered and guided like an exotic big game sport, the latest on record as recently as 1972. When one of the hunters was asked by a Swiss interviewer from the University of Bern what possible pleasure he derived from such macabre hunts of his fellow human beings, he answered, "Don't you know the skin of an Indian is tougher than any other for making hammocks?"

The Swiss, West German and British press ran stories. The London bureau chief of *The New York Times* was provided all possible evidence and information and agreed to give the story the prominence it deserved, but no story in the U.S. had yet appeared. In response to European outcries, the Stroessner government, through the President-for-life's personal press attaché, continued to deny all accounts of genocide, at the same time reaffirming its *committed war on Communism in the Americas* and *solidarity with the government of the United States in its war in Vietnam*. The Assistant Secretary for Inter-American Affairs of the United States State Department in

Washington then issued a statement: *We do not believe that there has been a planned or conscious effort on the part of the Government of Paraguay to exterminate, molest or harm Indians in any way. The unfortunate acts in remote areas seem to have been individual ones.*

Such was the Cold War era rhetoric, and what seemed rich meat for a free press journalist's meaningful story. The Stroessner government continued its program of wiping out indigenous peoples, forcing whole villages to migrate off their sacred homelands as exploited labor to wherever they were needed in a policy called *mandatory cooperation*. Multinational corporations such as Pennzoil, Pierre Schlumberger, Repsa, Phoenix Oil of Canada, Talent Oil of Canada, Carlos Casado, Unilever, Gulf & Western, Shell Oil—the list goes and on and on—were quickly moving into vacated tribal lands.

Against all of this, a resistance had been growing. Over the decades, tens of thousands of Guaraní-speaking exiles and refugees had been forced to flee across the three main rivers— the Río Paraná, Río Paraguay and Río Pilcomayo—into Argentina or Brazil, countries which, at least for a time, tolerated the exodus as part of campaigns to discredit Stroessner's policies of piracy and smuggling. Units formed up among these exiles, recently aided by logistical support and training from Cuba, and from other leftist insurgencies, becoming a perpetual barbed threat and danger to President-for-life Alfredo Stroessner's rule. The bands of *guerrilleros* crossed back across the rivers into Paraguay, into its thorn tree jungles, into grassy plains of its Chaco regions, where they ambushed government troops, robbed commercial river traffic and smugglers' barges, cut off the major roads, and staged hit-and-run actions all the way to the outskirts of the capital city of Asunción, their goal to destabilize and finally overthrow their tragic history of corrupt dictatorships in a rousing and exemplary Socialist revolution.

This resistance was currently being led by the *Ligas Agrarias Cristianas* (LACs) in the countryside, the *Organización Primero de Mayo* (OPM) in the villages and cities, militias with direct links to the Argentine leftist-Peronist guerrilla movement called *Montoneros*. *Montoneros-JP* was the group in which many of my friends from school and my adopted brothers in Buenos Aires were active members. In other words, war was brewing, simmering along in distant, land-locked Paraguay, a war which almost no one in the industrialized world had written about, or there was very little news I could find, in that era of laborious archival and card catalogue searches, that reached very far past Argentina and Brazil, which were facing their own armed struggles. In Paraguay—as with Guatemala's indigenous peasant insurgency, as with civil wars in El Salvador, in some ways as happened much later in Sandinista Nicaragua, and in Mexico's state of Chiapas—a guerrilla militia of enslaved peasants and repressed indigenous peoples had taken up arms *for the right to preserve their language and culture* and *for land reform and social democracy.*

These were the slogans, words with which journalism might tell the story. But as anyone who has written for any press soon learns, always searching for the right angle, brainstorming for that arresting lead, arguing with editors over the curse of *writing to space*, almost any story soon becomes remarkable for its omissions. Most journalism should be treated with contempt for the truth it conceals.

On the bank of the Río Pilcomayo, we took some time collecting ourselves. I checked through my shoulder bag to see that my cheap but pampered Pentax camera gear had made it through intact, pulling out the body and lenses to wipe off a heavy dampness that covered them like stubborn grease. Sikín busied himself pinching off a big liver-colored leech just above his sock. He checked me over for leeches. We felt over our bruises, splashing hydrogen peroxide on our scratches and cuts from a bottle Sikín carried in his bag. Then he looked around a bit for his hat, pissed off at himself for losing it crashing through the brush.

"Monkeys," he muttered. "Everything is out of balance."

And I wasn't sure what he meant by that, if it applied only to the forest or more generally, this wariness I sensed in him, like a bad omen. He started leading us upriver into mud that had the consistency of a red chocolate pudding. We sank to our knees at times, wading through the shallows. Once, he stopped, made a hand signal to me to freeze in place, quit my splashing. He listened—there might have been a distant humming sound, and I understood he was wary of helicopters—then he shook his head. We pressed on until we reached a graveled log landing that lay about fifty meters or so from where we had fled out of the trees, our intended destination had we been able to follow the log skidder trail to its end.

Waiting there, tied by a frayed rope to a black piling that leaned out of the water, was a square-nosed, plywood boat about thirty feet long, a third that size in the beam, dangerously listing, very low in the water, painted a faded chipped blue, washes of rust trails down its sides. This boat was packed tightly with heavy milk cans. They were the kind like big steel cream bottles, with pull-off lids, handles on both sides. Neat rows of these cans were packed together, taking up all available space, stainless steel flashing in the sun each time that sorry excuse for a boat—a crude barge, really—bobbed heavily up to its apex in the currents then lumbered down, low, until the river almost started spilling in over the sides.

We climbed awkwardly over the milk cans into this boat. Sikín worked at starting the engine, mounted under a crude wood box dead center. He had to lift a battered wood cover, pull off and put back some frayed-looking wires to a battery coated with corrosive white dust. The motor turned over, sputtered and gargled like a flushing toilet. Two balls of black grimy smoke spit up out of a rusty pipe and the engine finally kicked into life with a bone-jangling rattle. Sikín was supposedly a master of boats, expert at reading the river and its ever- shifting mud bars, an essential part of his job for the tree farms. *Compañeros* from the OPM had left this boatload of milk cans tied there for him the night before. He made this run every month or so. It was his job to take the cargo around the drifting dead-head logs, then pilot it across the river, dodging the mud bars, as if this were any local *indio* milk run in innocent light of day right under the noses of any military patrols, Paraguayan or Argentine army helicopters or border police in fast fiberglass cruisers armed with machine guns.

There wasn't much room for the two of us among all the milk cans. We had to straddle them, squeeze ourselves in between and step over them, no place at all to sit except on top of one, the steel handle uncomfortable. I sat down on one. Then I realized these cans might hold explosives. So I rode standing, swaying in between the heavy, unmoving milk cans, wondering how the weight of them all didn't break through what seemed like the too-flimsy plywood bottom of the boat. Water lapped over the toes of my boots, about three inches deep in the bilge. Sikín threw off the line. The engine strained, clattered in loud complaint. The boat very slowly pushed ahead, bobbing heavily out past the piling into reddish brown currents, engine noise too loud for us to speak to each other except in shouts.

Feeling the knots on my head swelling up, throbbing in rhythm to the engine noise with an intense headache that seemed to be peeling the scalp off the individual bones of my skull—experiencing flashbacks of dark flying shapes with quick little flips of panic and awe—still, I was getting excited, eagerly checking over my camera gear and tape recorder in my bag. Yes, for the fifth time, film was loaded, shutter speed and aperture set for high sun, tape recorder buttons ready with one push of my thumb. I fitted them back into my canvas bag that also contained two language texts, one Spanish and the one in Guaraní, underwear and socks, bottles of malaria pills, a spiral notebook, two cartons of cigarettes, a pint bottle of scotch I had drunk down halfway the night before to get what sleep I did. But here we were now, plowing along like riding on the back of a big wood and steel laden whale, at full screaming throttle only barely propelled, in a kind of directed drifting, out into deeper channels of the river, open water. And I was thinking, *This is it! Anything can happen! If Harry could only see me now!*

Ahead of us was the comb-with-missing-teeth line of green thorn trees appearing ever closer, the scrub jungle of Paraguay set into its red sandstone-colored earth. All of it seemed empty. We appeared to be the only thing moving on the sun-flickering water. In the far distance, some kind of great white bird, like a crane or a stork, rose lazily up, floating away, higher and higher, until it vanished into a sky so steamy pale blue, so chalky looking in the bright tropical sun the sky looked almost white. The thought struck me that this was what people meant when they said *the ends of the earth*, and how, barely a few years ago, when Harry and I walked shivering through grim winter streets in New York, homeless and miserable, locked out of anywhere we could sleep, this—*right here!*—was *precisely* the last place in the world I ever would have dreamed of being.

Yesterday, a woman asked me, *what was it like?*
Memory plays its tricks. The suddenness, the intensity of battle overwhelmed my senses. The trees, green density on the riverbank as we approached, began flying up, whole, and in bits and pieces. Branches, twigs, leaves scattered in the air, fluttering down all over and ahead of us with an eerie unreality like a slow-motion silent film full of green confetti—*it was like being in a movie.* There was detachment, not knowing what I was seeing, so that I perceived it all like I was inside a kind of animated cartoon, might even have laughed, turning to Sikín, trying to shout at him over the engine noise even as he was ducking down, taking cover behind the engine box, *Wow, what's that?*

Then *the reality of impact*, the boat bottom quaking up through my feet, a sudden shock jarring my whole body and buckling my knees like jumping from a small height, about ten feet or so, and landing, *hard*, only there had been no jump, this was a boat on a river. A huge orange flash, the sensation of *impact* first, followed by a big *pawhuuumpp!*—the mortar round hitting the riverbank. The boat bucked up under my feet. A stinging sandblast of hot wind and debris knocked me sprawling like a walloping hammer blow.

All of this happened at the same time, in scant fragments of a second. I was suddenly on my back, rolling over the milk cans, arms and legs reaching up and kicking helplessly. I heard a series of *pop-pop-pop* and *pop-pop pop* sounds over the boat engine, the *whizz-waanng* of ricochets, then a *ringggg!* Then I couldn't hear anymore, it was like my head was stuffed inside this big clanging bell. I sensed distantly, as by a consciousness hovering outside my body, *We're being shot at! Bullets are hitting the boat!* I'm not sure this was an actual thought at the time, it may only seem so in a memory of how I crashed around on top of those rib-breaker cans. Huge slaps of water broke over the boat, into my face, wetting me down like bucketsful. I was thinking, *This boat is going to sink!* But I couldn't do anything about it, as stunned as a stepped-on bug. What I could see was a blur of white sky. Then it was over, as I had said at the table when I rudely snapped my fingers, it was over like *that*.

The world turned quiet when the scream of the boat motor and all its vibrations shut off. I had to catch myself from pitching over the side as the bow hit the beach, the bottom grinding into mud. It was a blur how I gathered myself up and jumped out onto the bank, following Sikín, seeing everything at first as if not seeing anything. Then suddenly, *there it was*— war—bloody proof that each casualty bears witness to the existence of a special category of bullet, a unique personality for every knifelike piece of shrapnel. Casualties began appearing—dead, dying, wounded.

Fast movements, dozens of soldiers rushed past me on the beach with military purpose. Where had they come from? How hadn't I seen them? I became aware that I was walking in a strange way, lifting my legs too high, feet not exactly landing where I willed, like I was drunk, tottering to keep my balance. I was fighting hard to concentrate, hearing the voice of Ted Majeski, one of my old photo editors at UPI, *Learn how to see the scene in front of you, get the wide angle first then focus in and pick your shots.*

But I just staggered around, stupefied.

Sikín was waving the rebel soldiers on to the boat with high agitation, a panicked urgency, at the same time letting loose an angry streak of Guaraní at a *comandante* in a black beret with red star. The *comandante* had his pistol out, and he was speaking with it, the barrel jabbing at Sikín's face. Behind them, milk cans were being lifted out of the boat, two men needed for each, the caps pulled off, cans tilted over on the bank. Milk splashed out, flowed—*there was milk in them!* What looked like boxed and belted ammo, mortar rockets, grenades, other supplies were being pulled out of the cans, heavy packages wrapped in clear plastic bound with black tape, boxes with letters in the Cyrillic alphabet. Brown hands and arms reached in for supplies, came out dripping white with milk.

On the beach just up from the boat, rebel soldiers were being systematically loaded one after another with the supplies into heavy packs. They kept glancing nervously at the loud argument with their *comandante*—Sikín wasn't backing down. He pushed the *comandante's* pistol aside. He shouted, two inches from this commander's face. He made a quick move at his bag and pulled out his own gun. The two faced off like this, guns drawn, screaming.

Later, I learned how Sikín had been used, how he had been betrayed. Word was leaked from guerrilla command about this arms delivery so government soldiers would set up an ambush. The rebels—badly in need of a morale-boosting victory—had then ambushed the ambushers. From now on, Sikín would be a marked man along the river. If he didn't flee into exile, soon, he would be a victim of a death squad. He would be forced to take up arms and join the guerrillas in the jungle. He had no choice now. He would have to quit his job, abandon his family, or just wait to be killed. I knew nothing of this at the time.

Their argument subsided into calmer shouts, in Guaraní, like a loud singing.

I looked around. Wide angle: the guerrilla fighters, dozens of them, in ragged shorts, bare brown chests, some in filthy T-shirts, some in frayed straw hats, AK-47 assault rifles held out in front of them, pointing, as they were appearing out of the trees, eerily silent, faces hypervigilant but showing a restrained satisfaction, the grim relief of victory. Others came out of the trees further down the bank, herding about thirty government soldiers in clean khaki greens, billed campaign caps, hands on their heads. Shock and terror showed in their faces. The prisoners were being formed into a long irregular line, rebel soldiers moving down this line, stripping them of gear, starting with efficient use of their rifle butts to make each prisoner sit down in the mud and take off his boots. Rebels jabbed them in the ribs with gun barrels to hurry them.

Further up the bank, teams of guerrillas dragged green-uniformed casualties out of the trees, laying them out in a bloody row. Blood was everywhere, in long dragging trails. Rebel soldiers worked fast, stripping the bodies, starting with the boots. Blood splashed, sprayed up. A phrase in Spanish struck me with sudden clarity, a peasant euphemism for saying someone had died, *dejó los zapatos*—he left his shoes.

How close I got to them, I'm still not sure. Memory fails, revises, embellishes, everything replays itself each time differently like some horrible recurring dream. Maybe I didn't actually stand right over and look into the faces of the wounded, the dying, the dead, in their inconceivable suffering. Perhaps I didn't just stare dumbly, helplessly at them like some kind of vampire voyeur drawn to blood. I like to think I stood back some respectful distance, giving them a sacred privacy. Sometimes, I imagine I was crossing myself and praying, the way I was taught as a child, *All I really did that day was stand there crossing myself and praying.*

I wish I could say this. But I know it isn't true.

A government soldier with a missing finger, arm raised, twisted into a strange beckoning gesture—the bloody stump of his index finger pointed straight at me. He couldn't have been more than sixteen, such a clean-looking face where it wasn't covered by black crusts of blood. Stroessner's army drafted kids, teenagers, *indios* from the villages, or they were pressured to join by *economic necessity*, military service one of the only ways they might get their families out of poverty. In the green uniforms, they were all mostly *indio* kids. A special category of bullet had thought to cut off this one's right index finger as cleanly as if chopped by a cleaver. The bullet decided then to plow a red meaty furrow up his arm, coming out through his shoulder. From there, this bullet had taken an improbable leap, straight into his forehead. There was a leaking hole in one side of his forehead. His right eye socket was a deep gory hole, the eyeball blown out by the impact, stuck to his cheek by bloody strings. His other eye was half-closed. This gave him a sly look, a dark brown seduction, as in the Spanish expression, *¡Ojo!*, his last message to the living, *Watch out!*

We wouldn't see the wars that were coming. We wouldn't see the old strongman Juan Perón betraying us all, cracking down on the left wing with his police the moment he set foot back in Argentina. Then he would die in office, his regime replaced by a murderous military junta, their death squads kicking down the doors. Two of my adopted brothers in Argentina and one out of five of my friends would be carried off, hoods over their heads, hands wired behind their backs, held in secret jails, tortured, drugged, pushed still living out of airplanes flying at night over the Río de la Plata or the South Atlantic, *the disappeared*.

This would become my story—a *dirty war* that I had never imagined looking for would find me and my family. We wouldn't see ourselves staring into excavated mass graves, combing through refrigerated warehouses stacked with corpses waiting for identification or for forensic study for evidence of *crimes against humanity*. We wouldn't see ourselves marching with the mothers, *las madres*, in the plazas wearing white scarves over their heads, how they would hold up signs with photographs of the missing, my own adopted mother among them. We wouldn't see ourselves day after day year after year, searching through archives, police files, military records, interviews, legal transcripts, court testimony, making up lists, going over lists, printing lists, mailing lists, reading lists aloud, walking in reverence past granite walls engraved with lists, the lists of lists, lists of tens upon tens of thousands of their names.

Thorn trees were burning. From somewhere deep in the jungle, black smoke rose, drifting out over the river. The rebel soldiers were hurrying, running back and forth, splitting up their loot with increasing urgency.

I stumbled down the riverbank, along the row of dead and dying. Laid out next to the soldier who pointed at me with the stub of his finger, dumped there without his boots, like a compressed heavy lump of green, was a dead government soldier with an extra ear. Some hot knife of shrapnel had apparently cut off the ear of a soldier huddling close to him, then buried it in his throat—punched it in deep, like it was stapled there. It looked like a weirdly misassigned body part, this perfectly formed, undamaged shell of a human ear, like *a third ear* had just grown out from the shredded hamburger mess left of his throat. Death caught him like this, clutching at his throat with a fixed, glassy-eyed terror and stunned surprise. His legs were buckled, broken backwards at his hips, spread out in figure-fours under his body, bent like chicken wings. He must have been blown backwards at the waist by an impact while his legs stayed behind. He was a contortionist, this one, a real acrobat, bent completely in two, folded over that way, like compressed so he could have fit into a suitcase. Both arms were stiffening in this reaching spasm, hands not wanting to let go of his throat. His mouth was wide open like he had been trying to shout, as if his last alive move had been reaching for that alien ear choking off the source of his smothered voice.

Operation Condor drifted like the gigantic vulture it really was, on Cold War winds, hatched in secret policy-making rooms in Washington, fed and nurtured by the Pentagon, sent flying off down south on great silent wings, gliding along the isthmus of Central America to the Andes then out over the jungles, a hushed unified campaign of installing dictatorships everywhere, *juntas* of generals, puppet governments, rigged elections, *the Monroe doctrine, the war on Communism.* Latin American officer cadres and police units were invited first to bases in Panama then to Fort Benning, Georgia—the *School of the Americas* of the United States—where they were trained in the latest techniques of crowd control, electronic surveillance, leftist movement infiltration, mass arrest tactics, interrogation, torture, assassination, the *School of the Assassins,* as it became known to anyone who cared to listen. President-for-life Alfredo Stroessner would crush all opposition, kill off the guerrilla insurgencies not so much in pitched battles as with tactics of infiltration and death squads working in the nights. He would do this in coordination with fellow generals on all his borders, united together under the muffled flight of *Operation Condor.* Generals were heartened and empowered by recent success in

Chile, where a democratically elected government was overthrown and replaced with such tactics by a brutal military regime of human-rights criminal Agusto Pinochet, financed and supported by the United States. Death squad operations were inflicted on all opposition until they fled the country or were killed. They were killed by the thousands. Thousands died on all sides. As in the hollow propaganda of Pericles— may generations to come long forget him—the mangled dead were draped with words of glory.

Reports in the press had little effect to change such policies of terror. Most news became *the same news* almost everywhere, news people were willing to buy, *news consumer-surveyed for optimum market share.* Journalists disappeared. Voices from silence went unheard.

In Paraguay, President-for-Life Alfredo Stroessner continued freely his quiet campaign of genocide against Indians and suppression of the teaching of Guaraní in schools until, by the end of the century, indigenous peoples in his country could be counted on a few miserly nature preserves in fewer thousands than the old dictator had fingers and toes. *Palo trébol* trees, blue and gold macaws, countless exotic plant and animal species, half of the Paraná river basin—these would go extinct or nearly extinct, at most a few lonely specimens kept alive in greenhouses and zoos. A few native languages would be preserved at the odd university like tissue samples in formaldehyde. Demonstrations to raise awareness of such losses would be massive, with enthusiasm, the voices loud in protest, marches would turn into mobs would turn into riots smashing windows in cities, people died in the streets but few would hear them. The *union of growing productivity and growing destruction*, the *brinkmanship of annihilation*, the outcries of *poverty in the Third*

World, angry shouts against *the preservation of misery in the face of unprecedented wealth*—these voices went unheard.

Dictatorships outlived their usefulness, one after another replaced by *the new Latin American democracies*. President-for-Life Alfredo Stroessner would turn out not to be president for life. He would be ousted by a gentle coup, some said only by his blessing. He would be replaced by a "democracy" composed mostly of the same people in the *partido Colorado* who had been brought up under his regime. The same corruption, the same smuggling across rivers, the same 24-hour auto registration law, the same inexorable *policy of economic development* by energy companies, *the multinationals*, the same would continue under a different disguise, a brand new rhetoric, the new era of *the global marketplace, the privatization of state economies*. The *culture of corruption* remained the same—similarly in Argentina, Brazil, Peru, El Salvador, Ecuador, Panama, in Guatemala the same. In Colombia and Mexico, extortion, kidnapping and the *narcotraficantes* dominating the governments of states and localities were like an exponential multiplication of the same. Newly elected leaders lined their pockets then bolted office as fast as they could, one step ahead of criminal charges, those not quick enough or too arrogant to flee placed under house arrest. The same in Paraguay—all that would be required were new numbered bank accounts in Switzerland and Montevideo for depositing bribes.

Ex-President-for-Life Alfredo Stroessner, sage old general, would retire across the Río Paraguay to a fortress in Brazil, where he would be protected by new hired friends, an army of attorneys manipulating political asylum laws, fighting off his extradition for *crimes against humanity*. He would keep a guarded silence. As of yesterday, he was well into his 90s, enjoying a lucrative retirement. "He likes to go fishing and watch television," his personal assistant reports. "He plans to live to be a hundred."

Searching down the riverbank, I saw a government soldier with a missing ear getting his head wrapped in quickly bled-through bandages by the only guerrilla who wore something like a uniform—green khaki pants, fishing vest with bulging pockets full of first-aid supplies over a green T-shirt, on his head a black beret with a big red star. He was paler-skinned, not an *indio*, a bearded Cuban medic serving with the rebels, his Spanish clipped with swallowed word endings typical of a Cuban accent, his tone comforting and brotherly while wrapping the wound, talking his line of political conversion, *Come join us, compañero, life means nothing without justice, this will heal nicely, you might hear better than ever, if Che Guevara were still alive, I swear he'd put pictures of us on his walls.*

His words were lost on the shaved-head private, this miserable *pelado*. He sat hugging his knees, rocking back and forth, way beyond listening.

One of the guerrilla soldiers approached. The Cuban medic shook his head, taped off the bandage, left the wounded man to go on to the next. The rebel soldier knelt down and quickly pulled off the wounded man's boots.

Another government soldier had been left nearer the thorn trees, at the edge of the shade. He was doubled over on his side, clutching at a stomach wound, curling more and more into himself, into a fetal position. His uniform was black with blood. He was moaning, weakly, a high, tearing sound, like a child whines all alone in a distant room. His bare feet kicked out in quick convulsions. He quit making sounds. His left hand stretched, relaxed. A gold wedding ring glinted that the rebel soldiers hadn't seen. In a distant mud village, a young *indio* widow would find a *yatay* tree. She would sit under it and weep to the *urutaú*, the mournful gray bird.

Other soldiers lay in a disorderly group close to the trees, left in the shade to die. From each, down the slope of the river bank, blood like big spills of dark paint mixed into one big spreading stain.

The smell of blood was everywhere, heavy, iron-filled, vaguely fishy, unmistakably human. Nothing smells like it, not even the blood of other mammals. Blood smell hung in the air like a mist, it set off primitive autonomic nervous responses, an anxiousness, a quick pulse, impulses to fight or run, a strange metallic taste in the mouth that caused an involuntary watering-up with saliva—it was like sucking on a metal bottle cap, or like that mouthful of watering-up just before vomiting. The memory of this blood smell is almost as sickening now as it was then.

I was suddenly sick, fighting getting sick, holding my breath, letting it out, puffing, taking in more quick sharp breaths but catching at my right side each time. I felt a cutting pain there. I was dizzy, could hardly see. A delayed intense pain began coming and going, like I was being smashed in the ribs by the blunt head of an ax. It was getting harder to take each step, boots growing heavier, like pulling them out of sucking mud. I started back along the river bank in the direction I had come—looking for the commotion of rebel soldiers arranging the clanging empty milk cans back in the boat. I needed out of there. All I wanted was to go home.

I almost tripped over another soldier, barely catching myself before I fell on him. He had a clean, unshaved face, a pretty, girlish face. He glanced up at me with a quick fear, then I saw the other side of his face, half his lower jaw blown away. A jagged shred of jawbone was all that was left there, sharp white bone sticking out. This splinter of bone jerked up and down, in steady rhythm, like a heartbeat. The man's eyes rolled everywhere like he couldn't focus, then they fixed on me. He seemed to be asking for some kind of help, struggling to tell me something, hands reaching up, but he couldn't speak. His bright red tongue kept licking up and around, feeling the exposed row of his perfect white upper teeth—what was left of his teeth—everything else missing on that side. He made choking sounds. He gurgled blood. The shattered hinge of his jaw jerked up and down like a ticking clock. All I did was raise my hands at him like fending him away, backing off from the horror of him.

The beach was suddenly busier with movement, everyone hurrying. Only then did it strike me, *my camera, my tape recorder!*

What was I doing, standing there like some *fool*?

My hands were down rummaging into my shoulder bag, hearing my editor's voice again, *Get the wide angle, see what's in front of you, shoot first, ask questions later.*

Wide angle: the platoon of rebel soldiers not concerned with prisoners nearly finished with their work, like a bucket brigade, unloading supplies from the boat, loading them into packs, slinging them over their shoulders with the looted gear and weapons. The heap of empty cans was stacked in the boat. Sikín was hurrying the last one in. He looked up fearfully, searching the sky for enemy helicopters everyone knew must be coming. Smoke was getting heavier, settling over the river in a dirty gray layer.

Where was the *comandante* now to talk with him? Could I at least get a picture with his troops?

My hands were feeling around inside my bag, moving in their practiced automatic sequence from hundreds of times lifting up my camera to start shooting. But nothing felt right.

My fingers were wet, they were groping around in a busted-up jangle of metal bits and broken glass. I lifted my bag, a heavy shapelessness to it like it was filled with gravel. There was a huge hole in the bag, a long rent on one end and running around to the side like it had been slashed. Things were dropping out. I looked around and behind. Glass glittered. Shredded tobacco followed in a trail of my bloody footprints.

I looked in my bag. The pampered Pentax was completely crushed and mangled, like it had been stepped on, a worthless piece of tin, back sprung open, everything tangled in a gray snake of film. Lenses were smashed black shapes, loose empty rings. The tape recorder was in pieces. Tobacco was everywhere, like a carton of cigarettes had exploded. One of the books was ripped through its pages from end to end between its covers, bits of it and cigarette paper all over, fluttering out in shreds of white stars. Everything sparkled with shattered glass, everything crushed and jumbled in a mess. A sour dizzying breath of scotch hit me straight in the face.

My mind went blank. Without meaning to, I felt myself sinking to the ground. Everything around me turned to buzzing noise. Only later did I realize that I was also bleeding. My hands dripped blood, cut by glass. I had four fractured ribs on my right side, where the bag had been. Pain was only beginning to rise up out of initial numbness. It felt like a plate of sheet steel was cutting into the whole length of my ribs. My face was also bleeding from multiple lacerations from sand and gravel blown up by the mortar shell. For about a year, it would become a regular nightly routine with tweezers and antiseptic, picking out grains of stuff still working its way through the skin, breaking out in angry red bumps on my face. None of this registered at the time. The hot jungle sun crashed onto my head like cymbals. I reached that place of shock which is out of all time—the point where everything is continually present in consciousness, where the brain as such no longer exists—and I could have sat there forever in this deafened condition. I *did* sit there something like forever—I'm still sitting there in some way—though the best I've been able to put together, the actual time that passed from beginning to end of the battle is between fifteen and twenty minutes.

Up near the trees, the *comandante* of the guerrillas marched down the line of captured soldiers with his pistol. They were all sitting the same way in the mud, knees hugged to their chests, their feet bare. Their faces showed quick panic they fought to control, shaved heads snapping straight up, courageously waiting. The *comandante* raised his pistol and aimed—*Crack!*

The first soldier in line fell back with a muffled shout. He grabbed at himself, writhing in the mud, shot through his foot. This was their policy, to leave them alive as a *gift of the revolution*. But they shot them in the foot, shattering the arch so they couldn't fight again.

The *comandante* continued down the line.

Crack! Crack! Crack! Crack!...

He reached the last one. This one was different than the rest, one I hadn't noticed before, with a normal growth of short black hair, two black bars of insignia on his green shoulders, lighter skin, a more Spanish-looking face but not so different. He had a mustache covering his face that was still like the others, a mostly *indio* face, a fine-featured face like Sikín's, a face not unlike the *comandante's* face, more *criollo*, more Spanish, but all were Paraguayan faces. His face was serious, older than the others, a face set now with the authority and purpose of his military profession. It was a seasoned warrior's face making a point to appear unafraid. He knew the rules. He would have done the same, and more, if their fortunes were reversed. One commander to another, his face was saying, let's get it over with like two brave men, *por la patria.*

This captain looked off across the Río Pilcomayo, into another country. With a languid movement, and a kind of reluctant intimacy, the *comandante* of the guerrillas raised his pistol and fired. The body snapped to the side, head spouting blood like from a garden hose.

People sometimes ask me, *what was it like?*

What it is like: A *comandante* moving down a line of prisoners, shooting. Soldiers loading up supplies so they can go on killing. The wreckage in a bag, destroyed tools of a profession. Hands and arms lifting me, carrying me to a boat. All around me, wounded, dying, dead. A white sky. Burning thorn trees. Loss forever of a way to express love. Blood and milk flowing in swirls into a river.

My brother is doing fingertip pushups in his room.